Bambi

'Bambi' is known to millions of people through Walt Disney's famous film. This is the original story of the young Prince of the Forest, Bambi the deer; from his birth to his coming of age as a fully grown stag, his education in the ways of nature and his terrible fear of that most deadly of enemies – man.

Felix Salten's story is one of the most powerful and moving animal tales ever written – evoking the painful reality of the danger-filled lives of wild animals.

Felix Salten

BAMBI

A Life in the woods

Translated from the German by
Whittaker Chambers

Illustrated by Maurice Wilson

Piper Books
in association with
Jonathan Cape

First published in Great Britain in 1928 by Jonathan Cape
This Piper edition published 1988
by Pan Books Ltd
Cavaye Place, London SW10 9PG

9 8 7 6 5 4 3 2

ISBN 0 330 30105 5

Printed and bound in Great Britain by
Cox & Wyman Ltd, Reading

H<small>E</small> came into the world in the middle of the thicket, in one of those little, hidden forest glades which seem to be entirely open, but are really screened in on all sides. There was very little room in it, scarcely enough for him and his mother.

He stood there, swaying unsteadily on his thin legs and staring vaguely in front of him, with clouded eyes, which saw nothing. He hung his head, trembled a great deal, and was still completely stunned.

'What a beautiful child,' cried the magpie.

She had flown past, attracted by the deep groans the mother uttered in her labour. The magpie perched on a neighbouring branch. 'What a beautiful child,' she kept repeating. Receiving no answer, she went on talkatively, 'How amazing to think that he should be able to get right up and walk! How interesting! I've never seen the like of it before in all my born days.

7

Of course, I'm still young, only a year out of the nest, you might say. But I think it's wonderful. A child like that, hardly a minute in this world, and beginning to walk already! I call that remarkable. Really, I find that everything you deer do is remarkable. Can he run, too?'

'Of course,' replied the mother softly. 'But you must pardon me if I don't talk with you now. I have so much to do, and I still feel a little faint.'

'Don't put yourself out on my account,' said the magpie. 'I have very little time myself. But you don't see a sight like this every day. Think what a care and bother such things mean with us. The children can't stir once they are out of the egg, but lie helpless in the nest and require an attention, an attention, I repeat, of which you simply can't have any comprehension. What a labour it is to feed them, what a trouble to watch them. Just think for a moment what a strain it is to hunt food for the children and to have to be eternally on guard lest something happens to them. They are helpless if you are not with them. Isn't it the truth? And how long it is before they can move; how long it is before they get their feathers and look like anything at all.'

'Pardon,' replied the mother, 'I wasn't listening.'

The magpie flew off. 'A stupid soul,' she thought to herself, 'very nice, but stupid.'

The mother scarcely noticed that she was gone. She continued zealously washing her newly-born. She washed him with her tongue, fondling and caressing his body in a sort of warm massage.

The slight thing staggered a little. Under the strokes of her tongue, which softly touched him here and there, he drew himself together and stood still. His little red coat, that was still somewhat tousled, bore fine white spots, and on his

vague baby face there was still a deep, sleepy expression.

Round about grew hazel bushes, dogwoods, blackthorns and young elders. Tall sycamores, beeches and oaks wove a green roof over the thicket, and from the firm, dark-brown earth sprang fern fronds, wood-vetch and sage. Underneath, the leaves of the violets, which had already bloomed, and of the strawberries, which were just beginning, clung to the ground. Through the thick foliage, the early sunlight filtered in a golden web. The whole forest resounded with myriad voices, was penetrated by them in a joyous agitation. The wood-thrush rejoiced incessantly, the doves cooed without stopping, the blackbirds whistled, finches warbled, the field-mice chirped. Through the midst of these songs, the jay flew, uttering its quarrelsome cry, the magpie mocked them, and the pheasants cackled loud and high. At times the shrill exulting of a woodpecker rose above all the other voices. The call of the falcon shrilled, light and piercing, over the tree-tops, and the hoarse crow chorus was heard continuously.

The little fawn understood not one of the many songs and calls, not a word of the conversations. He did not even listen to them. Nor did he heed any of the odours which blew through the woods. He only heard the soft licking against his coat that washed him and warmed him and kissed him. And he smelled nothing but his mother's body near him. She smelled good to him and, snuggling closer to her, he hunted eagerly around and found nourishment for his life.

While he suckled, the mother continued to caress her little one. 'Bambi,' she whispered. Every little while she raised her head and, listening, snuffed the wind. Then she kissed her fawn again, reassured and happy.

'Bambi,' she repeated. 'My little Bambi.'

IN early summer the trees stood still under the blue sky, held their limbs outstretched and received the direct rays of the sun. On the shrubs and bushes in the undergrowth, the flowers unfolded their red, white and yellow stars. On some the seed pods had begun to appear again. They perched innumerable on the fine tips of the branches, tender and firm and resolute, and seemed like small, clenched fists. Out of the earth came whole troops of flowers like motley stars, so that the soil of the twilit forest floor shone with a silent, ardent, colourful gladness. Everything smelled of fresh leaves, of blossoms, of moist clods and green wood. When morning broke, or when the sun went down, the whole woods resounded with a thousand voices, and from morning till night, the bees hummed, the wasps droned, and filled the fragrant stillness with their murmur.

These were the earliest days of Bambi's life. He walked behind his mother on a narrow track that ran through the midst of the bushes. How pleasant it was to walk there. The thick foliage stroked his flanks softly and bent supply aside. The track appeared to be barred and obstructed in a dozen places and yet they advanced with the greatest ease. There were tracks like this everywhere running criss-cross through the whole woods. His mother knew them all and, if Bambi sometimes stopped before a bush as if it were an impenetrable green wall, she always found where the path went through, without hesitation or searching.

Bambi questioned her. He loved to ask his mother questions. It was the pleasantest thing for him to ask a question and then to hear what answer his mother would give. Bambi was never surprised that question after question should come into his mind continually and without effort. He found it perfectly natural, and it delighted him very much. It was very delightful, too, to wait expectantly till the answer came. If it turned out the way he wanted, he was satisfied. Sometimes, of course, he did not understand, but that was pleasant also because he was kept busy picturing what he had not understood, in his own way. Sometimes he felt very sure that his mother was not giving him a complete answer, was intentionally not telling him all she knew. And, at first, that was very pleasant, too. For then there would remain in him such a lively curiosity, such suspicion, mysteriously and joyously flashing through him, such anticipation, that he would become anxious and happy at the same time, and grow silent.

Once he asked, 'Whom does this trail belong to Mother?'

His mother answered, 'To us.'

Bambi asked again, 'To you and me?'

'Yes.'

'To us two?'

'Yes.'

'Only to us two?'

'No,' said his mother, 'to us deer.'

'What are deer?' Bambi asked, and laughed.

His mother looked at him from head to foot and laughed too. 'You are a deer and I am a deer. We're both deer,' she said. 'Do you understand?'

Bambi sprang into the air for joy. 'Yes, I understand,' he said. 'I'm a little deer and you're a big deer, aren't you?'

His mother nodded and said, 'Now you see.'

But Bambi grew serious again. 'Are there other deer besides you and me?' he asked.

'Certainly,' his mother said. 'Many of them.'

'Where are they?' cried Bambi.

'Here, everywhere.'

'But I don't see them.'

'You will soon,' she said.

'When?' Bambi stood still, wild with curiosity.

'Soon.' The mother walked on quietly. Bambi followed her. He kept silent, for he was wondering what 'soon' might mean. He came to the conclusion that 'soon' was certainly not 'now'. But he wasn't sure at what time 'soon' stopped being 'soon' and began to be a 'long while'. Suddenly he asked, 'Who made this trail?'

'We,' his mother answered.

Bambi was astonished. 'We? You and I?'

The mother said, 'Well, we ... we deer.'

Bambi asked, 'Which deer?'

'All of us,' his mother said sharply.

They walked on. Bambi was in high spirits and felt like leaping off the path, but he stayed close to his mother. Something rustled in front of them, close to the ground. The fern fronds and wood-lettuce concealed something that advanced in violent motion. A threadlike, little cry shrilled out piteously; then all was still. Only the leaves and the blades of grass shivered back into place. A ferret had caught a mouse. He came slinking by, slid sideways, and prepared to enjoy his meal.

'What was that?' asked Bambi excitedly.

'Nothing,' his mother soothed him.

'But,' Bambi trembled, 'but I saw it.'

'Yes, yes,' said his mother. 'Don't be fright-

ened. The ferret has killed a mouse.' But Bambi
was dreadfully frightened. A vast, unknown
horror clutched at his heart. It was long before
he could speak again. Then he asked, 'Why did
he kill the mouse?'

'Because,' his mother hesitated. 'Let us walk
faster,' she said as though something had just
occurred to her and as though she had forgotten
the question. She began to hurry. Bambi sprang
after her.

A long pause ensued. They walked on quietly
again. Finally Bambi asked anxiously, 'Shall we
kill a mouse, too, some time?'

'No,' replied his mother.

'Never?' asked Bambi.

'Never,' came the answer.

'Why not?' asked Bambi, relieved.

'Because we never kill anything,' said his
mother simply.

Bambi grew happy again.

Loud cries were coming from a young ash-
tree which stood near their path. The mother

went along without noticing them, but Bambi stopped inquisitively. Overhead two jays were quarrelling about a nest they had plundered.

'Get away, you murderer!' cried one.

'Keep cool, you fool,' the other answered, 'I'm not afraid of you.'

'Look for your own nests,' the first one shouted, 'or I'll break your head for you.' He was beside himself with rage. 'What vulgarity!' he chattered, 'What vulgarity!'

The other jay had spied Bambi and fluttered down a few branches to shout at him. 'What are you gawking at, you freak?' he screamed.

Bambi sprang away terrified. He reached his mother and walked behind her again, frightened and obedient, thinking she had not noticed his absence.

After a pause he asked, 'Mother, what is vulgarity?'

'I don't know,' said his mother.

Bambi thought a while; then he began again. 'Why were they both so angry with each other, Mother?' he asked.

'They were fighting over food,' his mother answered.

'Will we fight over food, too, some time?' Bambi asked.

'No,' said his mother.

Bambi asked, 'Why not?'

'Because there is enough for all of us,' his mother replied.

Bambi wanted to know something else. 'Mother,' he began.

'What is it?'

'Will we be angry with each other some time?' he asked.

'No, child,' said his mother, 'we don't do such things.'

They walked along again. Presently it grew light ahead of them. It grew very bright. The trail ended with the tangle of vines and bushes. A few steps more and they would be in the bright open space that spread out before them. Bambi wanted to bound forward, but his mother had stopped.

'What is it?' he asked impatiently, already delighted.

'It's the meadow,' his mother answered.

'What is a meadow?' asked Bambi insistently.

His mother cut him short. 'You'll soon find out for yourself,' she said. She had become very serious and watchful. She stood motionless, holding her head high and listening intently. She sucked in deep breathfuls of air and looked very severe.

'It's all right,' she said at last, 'we can go out.'

Bambi leaped forward, but his mother barred the way.

18

'Wait till I call you,' she said. Bambi obeyed at once and stood still. 'That's right,' said his mother, to encourage him, 'and now listen to what I am saying to you.' Bambi heard how seriously his mother spoke and felt terribly excited.

'Walking on the meadow is not so simple,' his mother went on. 'It's a difficult and dangerous business. Don't ask me why. You'll find that out later on. Now do exactly as I tell you. Will you?'

'Yes,' Bambi promised.

'Good,' said his mother, 'I'm going out alone first. Stay here and wait. And don't take your eyes off me for a minute. If you see me run back here, turn round then and run as fast as you can. I'll catch up with you soon.' She grew silent and seemed to be thinking. Then she went on earnestly, 'Run any way as fast as your legs will carry you. Run even if something should happen ... even if you should see me fall to the ground. ... Don't think of me, do you understand? No matter what you see or hear, start running at once and just as fast as you possibly can. Do you promise me to do that?'

'Yes,' said Bambi softly. His mother spoke so seriously.

She went on speaking. 'Out there if I should call you,' she said, 'there must be no looking around and no questions, but you must get behind me instantly. Understand that. Run without pausing or stopping to think. If I begin to run, that means for you to run too, and no stopping until we are back here again. You won't forget, will you?'

'No,' said Bambi in a troubled voice.

'Now I'm going ahead,' said his mother, and seemed to become calmer.

She walked out. Bambi, who never took his eyes off her, saw how she moved forward with slow, cautious steps. He stood there full of expectancy, full of fear and curiosity. He saw how his mother listened in all directions, saw her shrink together, and shrank together himself, ready to leap back into the thickets. Then his mother grew calm agan. She stretched herself. Then she looked around satisfied and called, 'Come.'

Bambi bounded out. Joy seized him with such tremendous force that he forgot his worries in a flash. Through the thicket he could see only the green tree-tops overhead. Once in a while he caught a glimpse of the blue sky.

Now he saw the whole heaven stretching far and wide and he rejoiced without knowing why. In the forest he had seen only a stray sunbeam now and then, or the tender, dappled light that played through the branches. Suddenly he was standing in the blinding hot sunlight whose boundless power was beaming upon him. He stood in the splendid warmth that made him shut his eyes but which opened his heart.

Bambi was as though bewitched. He was completely beside himself with pleasure. He was simply wild. He leaped into the air three, four, five times. He had to do it. He felt a terrible desire to leap and jump. He stretched his young limbs joyfully. His breath came deeply and easily. He drank in the air. The sweet smell of the meadow made him so wildly happy that he had to leap into the air.

Bambi was a child. If he had been a human child he would have shouted. But he was a young deer, and deer cannot shout, at least not the way human children do. So he rejoiced with his legs and with his whole body as he flung himself into the air. His mother stood by and was glad. She saw that Bambi was wild. She watched how he bounded into the air and fell again awkwardly, in one spot. She saw how he stared around him, dazed and bewildered, only to leap up over and over again. She understood that Bambi knew only the narrow deer tracks in the forest and how his brief life was used to the limits of the thicket. He did not move from one place because he did not understand how to run freely around the open meadow.

So she stretched out her forefeet and bent laughingly towards Bambi for a moment. Then she was off with one bound, racing around in a circle so that the tall grass stems swished.

Bambi was frightened and stood motionless. Was that a sign for him to run back to the thicket? His mother had said to him, 'Don't worry about me no matter what you see or hear. Just run as fast as you can.' He was going to turn around and run as she had commanded him to, but his mother came galloping up suddenly. She came up with a wonderful swishing sound and stopped two steps from him. She bent towards him, laughing as she had at first and cried, 'Catch me.' And in a flash she was gone.

Bambi was puzzled. What did she mean? Then she came back again running so fast that it made him giddy. She pushed his flank with her nose and said quickly, 'Try and catch me,' and fled away.

Bambi started after her. He took a few steps, Then his steps became short bounds. He felt as if he were flying without any effort on his part. There was a space under his hoofs, space under his bounding feet, space and still more space. Bambi was beside himself with joy.

The swishing grass sounded wonderful to his ears. It was marvellously soft and as fine as silk where it brushed against him. He ran round in a circle. He turned and flew off in a new circle, turned around again and kept running.

His mother was standing still, getting her breath again. She kept following Bambi with her eyes. He was wild.

Suddenly the race was over. He stopped and came up to his mother lifting his hoofs elegantly. He looked joyfully at her. Then they strolled contentedly side by side.

Since he had been in the open, Bambi had felt the sky and the sun and the green meadow with his whole body. He took one blinding, giddy glance at the sun, and he felt its rays as they lay warmly on his back.

Presently he began to enjoy the meadow with his eyes also. Its wonders amazed him at every step he took. You could not see the tiniest speck of earth the way you could in the forest. Blade after blade of grass covered every inch of the ground. It tossed and waved luxuriantly. It bent softly aside under every footstep, only to rise up unharmed again. The broad green meadow was starred with white daisies, with the thick, round red and purple clover blossoms and bright, golden dandelion heads.

'Look, look, Mother,' Bambi exclaimed. 'There's a flower flying.'

'That's not a flower,' said his mother, 'that's a butterfly.'

Bambi stared at the butterfly, entranced. It had darted lightly from a blade of grass and was fluttering about in its giddy way. Then Bambi saw that there were many butterflies flying in the air above the meadow. They seemed to be in a hurry and yet moved slowly, fluttering up and down in a sort of game that delighted him. They really did look like gay flying flowers that would not stay on their stems but had unfastened themselves in order to dance a little. They looked, too, like flowers that come to rest at sundown but have no fixed places and have to hunt for them, dropping down and vanishing as if they really had settled somewhere, yet always flying up again, a little way at first, then higher and higher, and always searching farther and farther because all the good places have already been taken.

Bambi gazed at them all. He would have loved to see one close by. He wanted to see one face out continually. The air was aflutter with them.

When he looked down at the ground again, he was delighted with the thousands of living things he saw stirring under his hoofs. They ran and jumped in all directions. He would see a wild swarm of them, and the next moment they had disappeared in the grass again.

'Who are they, Mother?' he asked.

'Those are ants,' his mother answered.

'Look,' cried Bambi, 'see that piece of grass jumping. Look how high it can jump!'

'That's not grass,' his mother explained, 'that's a nice grasshopper.'

'Why does he jump like that?' asked Bambi.

'Because we're walking here,' his mother answered, 'he's afraid we'll step on him.'

'O,' said Bambi, turning to the grasshopper who was sitting on a daisy, 'O,' he said again politely, 'you don't have to be afraid; we won't hurt you.'

'I'm not afraid,' the grasshopper replied in a quavering voice, 'I was only frightened for a moment when I was talking to my wife.'

'Excuse us for disturbing you,' said Bambi shyly.

'Not at all,' the grasshopper quavered. 'Since it's you, it's perfectly all right. But you never know who's coming and you have to be careful.'

'This is the first time in my life that I've ever been on the meadow,' Bambi explained; 'my mother brought me. . . .'

The grasshopper was sitting with his head lowered as though he were going to butt. He put on a serious face and murmured, 'That doesn't interest me at all. I haven't time to stand here gossiping with you. I have to be looking for my wife. Hopp!' And he gave a jump.

'Hopp!' said Bambi in surprise at the high jump with which the grasshopper vanished.

Bambi ran to his mother. 'Mother, I spoke to him,' he cried.

'To whom?' his mother asked.

'To the grasshopper,' Bambi said, 'I spoke to him. He was very nice to me. And I like him so much. He's so wonderful and green and you can see through his sides. They look like leaves, but you can't see through a leaf.'

'Those are his wings,' said his mother.

'O,' Bambi went on, 'and his face is so serious and wise. But he was very nice to me anyhow. And how he can jump! "Hopp!" he said, and he jumped so high I couldn't see him any more.'

They walked on. The conversation with the grasshopper had excited Bambi and tired him a little, for it was the first time he had ever spoken to a stranger. He felt hungry and pressed close to his mother to be nursed.

Then he stood quietly and gazed dreamily into space for a little while with a sort of joyous ecstasy that came over him every time he was nursed by his mother. He noticed a bright flower moving in the tangled grasses. Bambi looked more closely at it. No, it wasn't a flower, but a butterfly. Bambi crept closer.

The butterfly hung heavily to a grass stem and fanned its wings slowly.

'Please sit still,' Bambi said.

'Why should I sit still? I'm a butterfly,' the insect answered in astonishment.

'O, please sit still, just for a minute,' Bambi pleaded, 'I've wanted so much to see you close to. Please.'

'Well,' said the butterfly, 'for your sake I will, but not for long.'

Bambi stood in front of him. 'How beautiful you are,' he cried, fascinated, 'how wonderfully beautiful, like a flower.'

'What?' cried the butterfly, fanning his wings, 'did you say like a flower? In my circle it's generally supposed that we're handsomer than flowers.'

Bambi was embarrassed. 'O, yes,' he stammered 'much handsomer, excuse me, I only meant...'

'What ever you meant is all one to me,' the butterfly replied. He arched his thin body affectedly and played with his delicate feelers.

Bambi looked at him enchanted. 'How elegant you are,' he said. 'How elegant and fine! And how splendid and white your wings are!'

The butterfly spread his wings wide apart, then raised them till they folded together like an upright sail.

'O,' cried Bambi, 'I know that you are handsomer than the flowers. Besides, you can fly and the flowers can't because they grow on stems, that's why.'

The butterfly spread his wings. 'It's enough,' he said, 'that I can fly.' He soared so lightly that Bambi could hardly see him or follow his flight. His wings moved gently and gracefully. Then he fluttered into the sunny air.

'I only sat still that long on your account,' he

said, balancing in the air in front of Bambi. 'Now I'm going.'

That was how Bambi found the meadow.

IN the heart of the forest was a little glade that belonged to Bambi's mother. It lay only a few steps from the narrow trail where the deer went bounding through the woods. But no one could ever have found it who did not know the little passage leading to it through the thick bushes.

The glade was very narrow, so narrow that there was only room for Bambi and his mother, and so low that when Bambi's mother stood up her head was hidden among the branches. Sprays of hazel, furze, and dogwood, woven about each other, intercepted the little bit of sunlight that came through the tree-tops, so that it never reached the ground. Bambi had come into the world in this glade. It was his mother's and his.

His mother was lying asleep on the ground. Bambi had dozed a little, too. But suddenly he had become wide awake. He got up and looked around.

The shadows were so deep where he was that it was almost dark. From the woods came soft rustlings. Now and again the field-mice chirped. Now and again came the clear hammering of the woodpecker or the joyless call of a crow. Everything else was still, far and wide. But the air was sizzling in the midday heat so that you could hear it if you listened closely. And it was stiflingly sweet.

Bambi looked down at his mother and said, 'Are you asleep?'

No, his mother was not sleeping. She had awakened the moment Bambi got up.

'What are we going to do now?' Bambi asked.

'Nothing,' his mother answered. 'We're going to stay where we are. Lie down, like a good boy, and go to sleep.'

But Bambi had no desire to go to sleep. 'Come on,' he begged, 'let's go to the meadow.'

His mother lifted her head. 'Go to the meadow,' she said, 'go to the meadow now?' Her voice was so full of astonishment and terror that Bambi became quite frightened.

'Can't we go to the meadow?' he asked timidly.

'No,' his mother answered, and it sounded very final. 'No, you can't go now.'

'Why?' Bambi perceived that something mysterious was involved. He grew still more frightened, but at the same time he was terribly anxious to know everything. 'Why can't we go to the meadow?' he asked.

'You'll find out all about it later when you're bigger,' his mother replied.

'But,' Bambi insisted, 'I'd rather know now.'

'Later,' his mother repeated; 'you're nothing but a baby yet,' she went on tenderly, 'and we don't talk about such things to children.' She had grown quite serious. 'Fancy going to the meadow at this time of day. I don't even like to think of it. Why, it's broad daylight.'

'But it was broad daylight when we went to the meadow before,' Bambi objected.

'That's different,' his mother explained; 'it was early in the morning.'

'Can we only go there early in the morning?' Bambi was very curious.

His mother was patient. 'Only in the early morning or late evening,' she said, 'or at night.'

'And never in the daytime, never?'

His mother hesitated. 'Well,' she said at last, 'sometimes a few of us do go there in the daytime. ... But those are special occasions ... I can't just explain it to you, you are too young yet. ... Some of us do go there. ... But we are exposed to the greatest danger.'

'What kind of danger?' asked Bambi, all attention.

But his mother did not want to go on with the conversation. 'We're in danger and that's enough for you, my son. You can't understand such things yet.'

Bambi thought that he could understand everything except why his mother did not want to tell him the truth. But he kept silent.

'That's what life means for us,' his mother went on, 'though we all love the daylight, especially when we're young, we have to lie quiet all day long. We can only roam around from evening till morning. Do you understand?'

'Yes,' said Bambi.

'So, my son, we'll have to stay where we are. We're safe here. Now, lie down again and go to sleep.'

But Bambi didn't want to lie down. 'Why are we safe here?' he asked.

'Because all the bushes shield us,' his mother answered, 'and the twigs snap on the shrubs and the dry twigs crackle and give us warning. And last year's dead leaves lie on the ground and rustle to warn us, and the jays and the magpies keep watch so we can tell from a distance if anybody is coming.'

'What are last year's leaves?' Bambi asked.

'Come and sit beside me,' said his mother, 'and I will tell you.' Bambi sat down contentedly, nestling close to his mother. And she told him how the trees are not always green, how the sunshine and the pleasant warmth disappear. Then it grows cold, the frost turns the leaves yellow, brown and red, and they fall slowly so that the trees and bushes stretch their bare branches to the sky and look perfectly naked. But the dry leaves lie on the ground, and when a foot stirs them they rustle. Then someone is coming. O, how kind last year's dead leaves are! They do their duty so well and are so alert and watchful. Even in mid-summer there are a lot of them hidden beneath the undergrowth. And they give warning in advance of every danger.

Bambi pressed close against his mother. It was so cosy to sit there and listen while his mother talked.

When she grew silent he began to think. He thought it was very kind of the good old leaves to keep watch, though they were all dead and frozen and had suffered so much. He wondered just what that danger could be that his mother was always talking about. But too much thought tired him. Round about him it was still. Only the air sizzling in the heat was audible. Then he fell asleep.

ONE evening Bambi was roaming about the meadow again with his mother. He thought that he knew everything there was to see or hear there. But in reality it appeared that he did not know as much as he thought.

This time was just like the first. Bambi played touch with his mother. He ran around in circles, and the open space, the deep sky, the fresh air intoxicated him so that he became quite wild. After a while he noticed that his mother was standing still. He stopped short in the middle of a leap so suddenly that his four legs spread far

35

apart. To get his balance he bounded high into the air and then stood erect. His mother seemed to be talking to someone he couldn't make out through the tall grasses. Bambi toddled up inquisitively.

Two long ears were moving in the tangled grass stems close to his mother. They were greyish-brown and prettily marked with black stripes. Bambi stopped, but his mother said, 'Come here. This is our friend, the Hare. Come here like a nice boy and let him see you.'

Bambi went over. There sat the Hare looking like a very honest creature. At times his long spoonlike ears stood bolt upright. At others they fell back limply as though they had suddenly grown weak. Bambi became somewhat critical as he looked at the whiskers that stood out so stiff and straight on both sides of the Hare's mouth. But he noticed that the Hare had a very mild face and extremely good-natured features, and that he cast timid glances at the world from out of his big round eyes. The Hare really did look friendly. Bambi's passing doubts vanished immediately. But oddly enough, he had lost all the respect he originally felt for the Hare.

'Good evening, young man,' the Hare greeted him, with studied politeness.

Bambi merely nodded good evening. He didn't understand why, but he simply nodded. He was very friendly and civil, but a little condescending. He could not help it himself. Perhaps he was born that way.

'What a charming young prince,' said the Hare to Bambi's mother. He looked at Bambi attentively, raising first one spoon-like ear, then the other, and then both of them, and letting them fall again, suddenly and limply, which didn't please Bambi. The motion of the Hare's ears seemed to say, 'He isn't worth bothering with.'

Meanwhile the Hare continued to study Bambi with his big round eyes. His nose and his mouth with the handsome whiskers moved incessantly in the same way a man who is trying not to sneeze twitches his nose and lips. Bambi had to laugh.

The Hare laughed quickly, too, but his eyes grew more thoughtful. 'I congratulate you,' he said to Bambi's mother. 'I sincerely congratulate you on your son. Yes, indeed, he'll make a splendid prince in time. Anyone can see that.'

To Bambi's boundless surprise he suddenly sat straight on his hind legs. After he had spied all around with his ears stiffened and his nose constantly twitching, he sat down decently on all fours again. 'Now if you good people will excuse me,' he said at last, 'I have all kinds of things to do tonight. If you'll be so good as to excuse me . . .' He turned away and hopped off with his ears back so that they touched his shoulders.

'Good evening,' Bambi called after him.

His mother smiled. 'The good Hare,' she said; 'he is so suave and prudent. He doesn't have an easy time of it in this world.' There was sympathy in her voice.

Bambi strolled about a little and left his mother to her meal. He wanted to meet his friend again and he wanted to make new acquaintances, besides. For without being very clear himself what it was he wanted, he felt a certain expectancy. Suddenly at a distance, he heard a soft rustling on the meadow, and felt a quick, gentle step tapping the ground. He peered ahead of him. Over on the edge of the woods something was gliding through the grasses. Was it alive? No, there were two things. Bambi cast a quick glance at his mother but she wasn't paying attention to anything and had her head deep in the grass. But the game was going on on the other side of the meadow in a shifting circle exactly as Bambi himself had raced around before. Bambi was so excited that he sprang back as if he wanted to run away. Then his mother noticed him and raised her head.

'What's the matter?' she called.

But Bambi was speechless. He could not find

his tongue and only stammered, 'Look over there.'

His mother looked over. 'I see,' she said, 'that's my cousin, and sure enough she has a baby too, now. No, she has two of them.' His mother spoke at first out of pure happiness, but she had grown serious. 'To think that Ena has two babies,' she said, 'two of them.'

Bambi stood gazing across the meadow. He saw a creature that looked just like his mother. He hadn't even noticed her before. He saw that the grasses were being shaken in a double circle, but only a pair of reddish backs were visible like thin red streaks.

'Come,' his mother said, 'we'll go over. They'll be company for you.'

Bambi would have run, but as his mother walked slowly, peering to right and to left at every step, he held himself back. Still, he was bursting with excitement and very impatient.

'I thought we would meet Ena some time,' his mother went on to say. 'Where can she have been keeping herself? I thought. I knew she had one child, that wasn't hard to guess. But two of them! . . .'

At last the others saw them and came to meet them. Bambi had to greet his aunt, but his mind was entirely on the children.

His aunt was very friendly. 'Well,' she said to him, 'this is Gobo and that is Faline. Now you run along and play together.'

The children stood stock-still and stared at each other, Gobo close beside Faline and Bambi in front of him. None of them stirred. They stood and gaped.

'Run along,' said Bambi's mother, 'you'll soon be friends.'

'What a lovely child,' Aunt Ena replied, 'he is really lovely. So strong, and he stands so well.'

'O well,' said his mother modestly, 'we have to be content. But to have two of them, Ena . . .'

'O yes, that's all very well,' Ena declared; 'you know, dear, I've had children before.'

'Bambi is my first,' his mother said.

'We'll see,' Ena comforted her, 'perhaps it will be different with you next time, too.'

The children were still standing and staring at each other. No one said a word. Suddenly Faline gave a leap and rushed away. It had become too much for her.

In a moment Bambi darted after her. Gobo followed him. They flew around in a semi-circle, they turned tail and fell over each other. Then they chased each other up and down. It was glorious. When they stopped, all topsy-turvy and somewhat breathless, they were already good friends. They began to chatter.

Bambi told them how he talked to the nice grasshopper and the butterfly.

'Did you ever talk to the bee?' asked Faline.

No, Bambi had never talked to the bee. He did not even know who he was.

'I've talked to him often,' Faline declared, a little pertly.

'The jay insulted me,' said Bambi.

'Really,' said Gobo, astonished, 'did the jay treat you like that?' Gobo was very easily astonished and was extremely timid.

'Well,' he observed, 'the hedgehog stuck me in the nose.' But he only mentioned it in passing.

'Who is the hedgehog?' Bambi asked eagerly. It seemed wonderful to him to be there with friends, listening to so many exciting things.

'The hedgehog is a terrible creature,' cried Faline, 'full of long spines all over his body and very wicked!'

'Do you really think he's wicked?' asked Gobo. 'He never hurts anybody.'

'Is that so?' answered Faline quickly. 'Didn't he stick you?'

'O that was only because I wanted to speak to him,' Gobo replied, 'and only a little anyhow. It didn't hurt me much.'

Bambi turned to Gobo. 'Why didn't he want you to talk to him?' he asked.

'He doesn't talk to anybody,' Faline interrupted, 'even if you just come where he is he rolls himself up so he's nothing but prickles all over. Our mother says he's one of those people who don't want to have anything to do with the world.'

'Maybe he's only afraid,' Gobo said.

But Faline knew better. 'Mother says you shouldn't meddle with such people,' she said.

Presently Bambi began to ask Gobo softly, 'Do you know what "danger" means?'

Then they both grew serious and all three heads drew together. Gobo thought a while. He made a special effort to remember, for he saw how curious Bambi was for the answer. 'Danger,' he whispered, 'is something very bad.'

'Yes,' Bambi declared excitedly, 'I know it's something very bad, but what?' All three trembled with fear.

Suddenly Faline cried out loudly and joyfully, 'I know what danger is, – it's what you run away from.' She sprang away. She couldn't bear to stay there any longer and be frightened. In an instant, Bambi and Gobo had bounded after her. They began to play again. They tumbled in the rustling, silky green meadow grass, and in a twinkling had forgotten all about the absorbing question. After a while they stopped and stood chattering together as before. They looked towards their mothers. They were standing close together, eating a little and carrying on a quiet conversation.

Aunt Ena raised her head and called the children. 'Come, Gobo. Come, Faline. We have to go now.'

And Bambi's mother said to him, 'Come, it's time to go.'

'Wait just a little longer,' Faline pleaded eagerly, 'just a little while.'

'Let's stay a little longer, please,' Bambi pleaded, 'it's so nice.' And Gobo repeated timidly, 'It's so nice, just a little longer.' All three spoke at once.

Ena looked at Bambi's mother. 'What did I tell you,' she said, 'they won't want to separate now.'

Then something happened that was much more exciting than everything else that happened to Bambi that day. Out of the woods came the sound of hoofs beating the earth. Branches snapped, the boughs rustled, and before Bambi had time to listen, something burst out of the thicket. Someone came crashing and rustling with someone else rushing after him. They tore by like the wind, described a wide circle on the meadow and vanished into the woods again, where they could be heard galloping. Then they came bursting out of the thicket again and suddenly stood still, about twenty paces apart.

Bambi looked at them and did not stir. They looked like his mother and Aunt Ena. But their heads were crowned with gleaming antlers covered with brown beads and bright white prongs. Bambi was completely overcome. He looked from one to the other. One was smaller and his antlers narrower. But the other one was stately and beautiful. He carried his head up and his antlers rose high above it. They flashed from dark to light, adorned with the splendour of many black and brown beads and the gleam of the branching white prongs.

'O,' cried Faline in admiration. 'O,' Gobo repeated softly. But Bambi said nothing. He was entranced and silent. Then they both moved and, turning, away from each other, walked

slowly back into the woods in opposite directions. The stately stag passed close to the children and Bambi's mother and Aunt Ena. He passed by in silent splendour, holding his noble head royally high and honouring no one with so much as a glance.

The children did not dare to breathe till he had disappeared into the thicket. They turned to look after the other one, but at that very moment the green door of the forest closed on him.

Faline was the first to break silence. 'Who were they?' she cried. But her pert little voice trembled.

'Who were they?' Gobo repeated in a hardly audible voice. Bambi kept silent.

Aunt Ena said solemnly, 'Those were your fathers.'

Nothing more was said, they parted. Aunt Ena led her children into the nearest thicket. It was her trail. Bambi and his mother had to cross the whole meadow to the oak in order to reach their own path. He was silent for a long time before he finally asked, 'Didn't they see us?'

His mother understood what he meant and replied, 'Of course, they saw all of us.'

Bambi was troubled. He felt shy about asking questions, but it was too much for him. 'Then why . . .' he began, and stopped.

His mother helped him along. 'What is it you want to know, son?' she asked.

'Why didn't they stay with us?'

'They don't ever stay with us,' his mother answered, 'only at times.'

Bambi continued, 'But why didn't they speak to us?'

His mother said, 'They don't speak to us now; only at times. We have to wait till they come to us. And we have to wait for them to speak to us. They do it whenever they like.'

With a troubled heart, Bambi asked, 'Will my father speak to me?'

'Of course he will,' his mother promised. 'When you're grown up he'll speak to you, and you'll have to stay with him sometimes.'

Bambi walked silently beside his mother, his whole mind filled with his father's appearance. 'How handsome he is!' he thought over and over again. 'How handsome he is!'

As though his mother could read his thoughts, she said, 'If you live, my son, if you are cunning and don't run into danger, you'll be as strong and handsome as your father is some time, and you'll have antlers like his, too.'

Bambi breathed deeply. His heart swelled with joy and expectancy.

Time passed, and Bambi had many adventures and went through many experiences. Every day brought something new. Sometimes he felt quite giddy. He had so incredibly much to learn.

He could listen now, not merely hear, when things happened so close that they struck the ear of their own accord. No, there was really no art in that. He could really listen intelligently now to everything that stirred, no matter how softly. He heard even the tiniest whisper that the wind brought by. For instance, he knew that a pheasant was running through the next bushes. He recognized clearly the soft quick tread that was always stopping. He knew by ear the sound the field-mice make when they run to and fro on their little paths. And the patter of the moles when they are in a good humour and chase one another around the elder bushes so that there is just the slightest rustling. He heard the shrill clear call of the falcon and he knew from its altered, angry tones when a hawk or an eagle approached. The falcon was angry because she was afraid her field would be taken from her. He knew the beat of the wood doves' wings, the beautiful, distant, soaring cries of ducks, and many other things besides.

He knew how to snuff the air now, too. Soon he would do it as well as his mother. He could breathe in the air and at the same time analyse it with his senses. 'That's clover and meadow grass,' he would think when the wind blew off the fields. 'And Friend Hare is out there, too. I can smell him plainly.'

Again he would notice through the smell of leaves and earth, wild leek and wood mustard, that the ferret was passing by. He could tell by putting his nose to the ground and snuffing deeply that the fox was afoot. Or he would know that one of his family was somewhere near by. It might be Aunt Ena and the children.

By now he was good friends with the night and no longer wanted to run about so much in broad daylight. He was quite willing to lie all day long in the shade of the leafy glade with his mother. He would listen to the air sizzling in the heat and then fall asleep.

From time to time, he would wake up, listen and snuff the air to find out how things stood. Everything was as it should be. Only the field-mice were chattering a little to each other, the midges who were hardly ever still, hummed, while the wood doves never ceased declaiming their ecstatic tenderness. What concern was it of his? He would drop off to sleep again.

He liked the night very much now. Everything was alive, everything was in motion. Of course, he had to be cautious at night too, but still he could be less careful. And he would go wherever he wanted to. And everywhere he went he met acquaintances. They too were always less nervous than in the daytime.

At night the woods were solemn and still. There were only a few voices. They sounded loud in the stillness, and they had a different ring from daytime voices, and left a deeper impression.

Bambi liked to see the owl. She had such a wonderful flight, perfectly light and perfectly noiseless. She made as little sound as a butterfly, and yet she was so dreadfully big. She had such striking features, too, so pronounced and so deeply thoughtful. And such wonderful eyes! Bambi admired her firm, quietly courageous glance. He liked to listen when she talked to his mother or to anybody else. He would stand a little to one side, for he was somewhat afraid of the masterful glance that he admired so much. He did not understand most of the clever things she said, but he knew they were clever, and they pleased him and filled him with respect for the owl.

Then the owl would begin to hoot. 'Hoaah! – Ha! – Ha! – Haa – ah!' she would cry. It sounded different from the thrushes' song, or the yellow-birds', different from the friendly notes of the cuckoo, but Bambi loved the owl's cry, for he felt its mysterious earnestness, its unutterable wisdom and strange melancholy.

Then there was the screech-owl, a charming little fellow, lively and gay with no end to his inquisitiveness. He was bent on attracting attention. 'Oi yeek! oi yeek!' he would call in a terrible, high-pitched, piercing voice. It sounded as if he were on the point of death. But he was really in a beaming good humour and was hilariously happy whenever he frightened anybody. 'Oi! yeek!' he would cry so dreadfully loud that the forests heard it for a mile around. But afterwards he would laugh with a soft chuckle, though you could only hear it if you stood close by.

Bambi discovered that the screech-owl was delighted whenever he frightened anyone, or when anybody thought that something dreadful had happened to him. After that, whenever Bambi met him, he never failed to rush up and ask, 'What has happened to you?' or to say with

a sigh, 'O, how you frightened me just now!'
Then the owl would be delighted.

'O, yes,' he would say, laughing, 'it sounds
pretty gruesome.' He would puff up his feathers
into a greyish-white ball and looked extremely
handsome.

There were storms, too, once or twice, both
in the daytime and at night. The first was in the
daytime and Bambi felt himself grow terrified
as it became darker and darker in his glade. It
seemed to him as if night had covered the sky at
mid-day. When the raging storm broke through
the woods so that the trees began to groan
aloud, Bambi trembled with terror. And when
the lightning flashed and the thunder growled,
Bambi was numb with fear and thought the end
of the world had come. He ran behind his
mother, who had sprung up somewhat disturbed and was walking back and forth in the
thicket. He could not think about nor understand
anything. The rain fell in raging torrents. Everyone had run to shelter. The woods were empty.
But there was no escaping the rain. The pouring water penetrated even the thickest parts of
the bushes. Presently the lightning stopped,
and the fiery rays ceased to flicker through the
tree-tops. The thunder rolled away. Bambi could
hear it in the distance, and soon it stopped altogether. The rain beat more gently. It pattered

evenly and steadily around him for another hour. The forest stood breathing deeply in the calm and let the water drain off. No one was afraid to come out any more. That feeling had passed. The rain had washed it away.

Never before had Bambi and his mother gone to the meadow as early as on that evening. It was not even dusk yet. The sun was still high in the sky, the air was extremely fresh, and smelt sweeter than usual, and the woods rang with a thousand voices, for everyone had crept out of his shelter and was running about excitedly, telling what had just happened.

Before they went on to the meadow, they passed the great oak that stood near the forest's edge, close to their trail. They always had to pass that beautiful big tree when they went to the meadow.

This time the squirrel was sitting on a branch and greeted them. Bambi was good friends with the squirrel. The first time he met him he took him for a very small deer because of the squirrel's red coat and stared at him in surprise. But Bambi had been very childish at that time and had known nothing at all.

The squirrel pleased him greatly from the first. He was so thoroughly civil, and talkative. And Bambi loved to see how wonderfully he could turn, and climb, and leap, and balance himself. In the middle of a conversation the squirrel would run up and down the smooth tree trunk as though there were nothing to it. Or he would sit upright on a swaying branch, balance himself comfortably with his bushy tail, that stuck up so gracefully behind him, display his white chest, hold his little forepaws elegantly in front of him, nod his head this way and that, laugh with his jolly eyes, and, in a twinkling, say a lot of comical and interesting things. Then he would come down again, so swiftly and with such leaps, that you expected him to tumble on his head.

He switched his long tail violently and called to them from overhead, 'Good day! Good day!

It's so nice of you to come over.' Bambi and his mother stopped.

The squirrel ran down the smooth trunk. 'Well,' he chattered, 'did you get through it all right? Of course, I see that everything is first-rate. That's the main thing.'

He ran up the trunk again like lightning and said, 'It's too wet for me down there. Wait, I'm going to look for a better place. I hope you don't mind. Thanks, I knew you wouldn't. And we can talk just as well from here.'

He ran back and forth along a straight limb. 'It was a bad business,' he said, 'a monstrous uproar! You wouldn't believe how scared I was. I hunched myself up as still as a mouse in the corner and hardly dared move. That's the worst of it, having to sit there and not move. And all the time you're hoping nothing will happen. But my tree is wonderful in such cases. There's no denying it, my tree is wonderful. I'll say that for it. I'm satisfied with it. As long as I've had it, I've never wanted any other. But when it cuts loose the way it did today you're sure to get frightened no matter where you are.'

The squirrel sat up balancing himself with his handsome upright tail. He displayed his white chest and pressed both forepaws protestingly against his heart. You believed without his adding anything that he had been excited.

'We're going to the meadow now to dry ourselves off in the sun,' Bambi's mother said.

'That's a good idea,' cried the squirrel, 'you're really so clever. I'm always saying how clever you are.' With a bound he sprang on to a higher branch. 'You couldn't do anything better than go to the meadow now,' he called down. Then he swung with light bounds back and forth through the tree-top. 'I'm going up where I can get the sunlight,' he chattered merrily, 'I'm all soaked through. I'm going all the way up.' He didn't care whether they were still listening to him or not.

The meadow was full of life. Friend Hare was there and had brought along his family. Aunt Ena was there with her children and a few acquaintances. That day Bambi saw the fathers again. They came slowly out of the forest from opposite directions. There was a third stag too. Each walked slowly in his track, back and forth along the meadow. They paid no attention to anyone and did not even talk to one another. Bambi looked at them frequently. He was respectful, but full of curiosity.

Then he talked to Faline and Gobo and a few other children. He wanted to play a while. All agreed and they began running around in a circle. Faline was the gayest of all. She was so fresh and nimble and brimming over with bright ideas. But Gobo was soon tired. He had been terribly frightened by the storm. His heart had hammered loudly and was still pounding. There was something very weak about Gobo, but Bambi liked him, because he was so good and willing and always a little sad without letting you know it.

Time passed and Bambi was learning how good the meadow grass tasted, how tender and sweet the leaf buds and the clover were. When he nestled against his mother for comfort it often happened that she pushed him away.

'You aren't a little baby any more,' she would say. Sometimes she even said abruptly, 'Go away and let me be.' It even happened sometimes that his mother got up in the little forest glade, got up in the middle of the day, and went off without noticing whether Bambi was following her or not. At times it seemed when they were wandering down the familiar paths, as if his mother did not want to notice whether Bambi was behind her or was trailing after.

One day his mother was gone. Bambi did not know how such a thing could be possible; he could not figure it out. But his mother was gone and for the first time Bambi was left alone.

He wandered about, he was troubled, he grew worried and anxious and began to want her terribly. He stood quite sadly, calling her. Nobody answered and nobody came.

He listened and snuffed the air. He could not smell anything. He called again. Softly, pathetically, tearfully, he called 'Mother, Mother!' In vain.

Then despair seized him, he could not stand it, and started to walk.

He wandered down the trails he knew, stopping and calling. He wandered farther and farther with hesitating steps, frightened and helpless. He was very downcast.

He went on and on and came to trails where he had never been before. He came to places that were strange to him. He no longer knew where he was going.

Then he heard two childish voices like his own, calling, 'Mother, Mother!' He stood still and listened. Surely that was Gobo and Faline. It must be they.

He ran quickly towards the voices and soon he saw their little red jackets showing through the leaves. Gobo and Faline were standing side by side under a dog-wood tree and calling mournfully, 'Mother, Mother!'

They were overjoyed when they heard the rustling in the bushes. But they were disappointed when they saw Bambi. They were a little consoled that he was there, however. And Bambi was glad not to be all alone any more.

'My mother is gone,' Bambi said.

'Ours is gone too,' Gobo answered plaintively.

They looked at one another and were quite despondent.

'Where can they be?' asked Bambi. He was almost sobbing.

'I don't know,' sighed Gobo. His heart was pounding and he felt miserable.

Suddenly Faline said, 'I think they may be with our fathers.'

Gobo and Bambi looked at her surprised. They were filled with awe. 'You mean that they're visiting our fathers?' asked Bambi, and trembled. Faline trembled too but she made a wise face. She acted like a person who knows more than she will let on. Of course she knew nothing, she could not even guess where her idea came from. But when Gobo repeated, 'Do you really think so?' she put on a meaningful air and answered mysteriously, 'Yes, I think so.'

Anyway it was a suggestion that needed to be thought about. But in spite of that Bambi felt no easier. He couldn't even think about it, he was too troubled and too sad.

He went off. He wouldn't stay in one place. Faline and Gobo went along with him for a little way. All three were calling, 'Mother, Mother!' Then Gobo and Faline stopped; they did not dare go any farther. Faline said, 'Why should we? Mother knows where we are. Let's stay here so she can find us when she comes back.'

Bambi went on alone. He wandered through a thicket to a little clearing. In the middle of the clearing Bambi stopped short. He suddenly felt as if he were rooted to the ground and could not move.

On the edge of the clearing, by a tall hazel bush, a creature was standing. Bambi had never seen such a creature before. At the same time the air brought him a scent such as he had never smelled in his life, It was a strange smell, heavy and acrid. It excited him to the point of madness.

Bambi stared at the creature. It stood remarkably erect. It was extremely thin and had a pale face, entirely bare around the nose and the eyes. A kind of dread emanated from that face, a cold terror. That face had a tremendous power over him. It was unbearably painful to look at that face and yet Bambi stood staring fixedly at it.

For a long time the creature stood without moving. Then it stretched out a leg from high up near its face. Bambi had not even noticed that there was one there. But as that terrible leg was reaching out into the air Bambi was swept away by the mere gesture. In a flash he was back into the thicket he came from, and was running away.

In a twinkling his mother was with him again, too. She bounded beside him over shrubs and bushes. They ran side by side as fast as they could. His mother was in the lead. She knew the way and Bambi followed. They ran till they came to their glade.

'Did you see Him?' asked the mother softly.

Bambi could not answer, he had no breath left. He only nodded.

'That was He,' said the mother.

And they both shuddered.

Bambi was often alone now. But he was not so troubled about it as he had been the first time. His mother would disappear and no matter how much he called her she wouldn't come back. Later she would appear unexpectedly and stay with him as before.

One night he was roaming around quite forlorn again. He could not even find Gobo and Faline. The sky had become pale grey and it began to darken so that the tree-tops seemed like a vault over the bushy undergrowth. There was a swishing in the bushes, a loud rustling came through the leaves and Bambi's mother dashed out. Someone else raced close behind her. Bambi did not know whether it was Aunt Ena or his father or someone else. But he recognized his mother at once. Though she rushed past him so quickly, he had recognized her voice. She screamed and it seemed to Bambi as if it were in play, though he thought it sounded a little frightened too.

eyes so that I can't see at all, and my heart beats
so fast that I can't breathe.'

Faline became very thoughtful after Bambi's
story and did not say anything.

But the next time they met, Gobo and Faline bounded up in great haste. They were alone again and so was Bambi. 'We have been hunting for you all this time,' cried Gobo. 'Yes,' Faline said importantly, 'because now we know who it was you saw.' Bambi bounded into the air for curiosity and asked, 'Who?'

Faline said solemnly, 'It was the old Prince.'

'Who told you that?' Bambi demanded.

'Mother,' Faline replied.

Bambi was amazed. 'Did you tell her the whole story?' They both nodded. 'But it was a secret,' Bambi cried angrily.

Gobo tried to shield himself at once. 'I didn't do it, it was Faline,' he said. But Faline cried excitedly 'What do you mean, a secret? I wanted to know who it was. Now we all know and it's much more exciting.'

Bambi was burning up with desire to hear all about it and let himself be mollified. Faline told him everything. 'The old Prince is the biggest stag in the whole forest. There isn't anybody else that compares with him. Nobody knows how old he is. Nobody can find out where he lives. No one knows his family. Very few have seen him even once. At times he was thought to be dead because he hadn't been seen for so long. Then someone would see him again for a second and so they knew he was still alive. Nobody had ever dared ask him where he had been. He speaks to nobody and no one dares speak to him. He uses trails none of the others ever use. He knows the very depths of the forest. And he does not know such a thing as danger. Other Princes fight one another at times, sometimes in fun or to try each other out, sometimes in earnest. For many years no one has fought with the old stag. And of those who fought with him long ago not one is living. He is the great Prince.'

Bambi forgave Gobo and Faline for babbling his secret to their mother. He was even glad to have found out all these important things, but he was glad that Gobo and Faline did not know all about it. They did not know what the great Prince had said, 'Can't you stay by yourself? Shame on you!' Now Bambi was very glad that he had not told them about these things. For then Gobo and Faline would have told that along with the rest, and the whole forest would have gossiped about it.

That night when the moon rose Bambi's mother came back again. He suddenly saw her standing under the great oak at the edge of the meadow looking around for him. He saw her right away and ran to her.

That night Bambi learned something new. His mother was tired and hungry. They did not walk as far as usual. The mother quieted her hunger in the meadow where Bambi too was used to eating most of his meals. Side by side they nibbled at the bushes and pleasantly ruminating, went farther and farther into the woods.

Presently there was a loud rustling in the bushes. Before Bambi could guess what it was his mother began to cry aloud as she did when she was very terrified or when she was beside herself. 'Aoh!' she cried and, giving a bound, stopped and cried, 'Aoh! Baoh!' Bambi tried to make out the mighty forms which were drawing near as the rustling grew louder. They were right near now. They resembled Bambi and Bambi's mother, Aunt Ena and all the rest of his family, but they were gigantic and so powerfully built that he stared up at them overcome.

Suddenly Bambi began to bleat, 'Aoh! Baoh-baoh!' He hardly knew he was bleating. He couldn't help himself. The procession tramped slowly by. Three, four giant apparitions, one after the other. The last of them was bigger than any of the others. He had a wild mane on his neck and his antlers were tree-like. It took Bambi's breath away to see them. He stood and bleated from a heart full of wonder, for he was more weirdly affected than ever before in his life. He was afraid, but in a peculiar way. He felt how pitifully small he was, and even his mother seemed to him to have shrunk. He felt

ashamed without understanding why and at the
same time terror shook him. He bleated, 'Baoh!
b-a-o-h!' He felt better when he bleated that
way.

The procession had gone by. There was nothing more to be seen or heard. Even his mother
was silent. Only Bambi kept giving short bleats
now and then. He still felt the shock.

'Be still,' his mother said, 'they have gone
now.'

'Oh, Mother.' Bambi whispered, 'who was
it?'

'Well,' said his mother, 'they are not so dangerous when all is said and done. Those are your
big cousins, the elk – they are strong and they

are important, far stronger than we are.'

'And aren't they dangerous?' Bambi asked.

'Not as a rule,' his mother explained. 'Of course, a good many things are said to have happened. This and that is told about them, but I don't know if there is any truth in such gossip or not. They've never done any harm to me or to any one of my acquaintances.'

'Why should they do anything to us?' asked Bambi, 'if they are cousins of ours?' He wanted to feel calm but he kept trembling.

'O, they never do anything to us,' his mother answered, 'but I don't know why, I'm frightened whenever I see them. I don't understand it myself. But it happens that way every time.'

Bambi was gradually reassured by her words but he remained thoughtful. Right above him in the branches of an elder, the screech-owl was hooting in his blood-curdling way. Bambi was distracted and forgot to act as if he had been frightened. But the screech-owl flew by anyhow and asked, 'Didn't I frighten you?'

'Of course,' Bambi replied, 'you always frighten me.'

The screech-owl chuckled softly. He was pleased. 'I hope you don't hold it against me,' he said, 'it's just my way.' He fluffed himself up so that he resembled a ball, sank his bill in his foamy white feathers and put on a terribly wise

70

and serious face. He was satisfied with himself.

Bambi poured out his heart to him. 'Do you know?' he began slyly, 'I've just had a much worse fright.'

'Indeed!' said the owl, displeased.

Bambi told him about his encounter with his giant relations.

'Don't talk to me about relations,' the owl exclaimed, 'I've got relations too. But I only fly about in the daytime so they are all down on me now. No, there isn't much use in relations. If they're bigger than you are, they're no good to you, and if they're smaller they're worth still less. If they're bigger than you, you can't bear them because they're proud, and if they're smaller they can't bear you because you're proud. No, I prefer to have nothing to do with the whole crowd.'

'But I don't even know my relations,' Bambi said, laughing shyly. 'I never heard of them, I never saw them, before today.'

'Don't bother about such people,' the screech-owl advised. 'Believe me,' and he rolled his eyes significantly, 'believe me, it's the best way. Relatives are never as good as friends. Look at us, we're not related in any way but we're good friends, and that's much better.'

Bambi wanted to say something else but the screech-owl went on, 'I've had experience with such things. You are still too young but, believe me, I know better. Besides, I don't like to get mixed up in family affairs.' He rolled his eyes thoughtfully and looked so impressive with his serious face that Bambi kept a discreet silence.

Another night passed and morning brought an event.

It was a cloudless morning, dewy and fresh. All the leaves on the trees and the bushes seemed suddenly to smell sweeter. The meadows sent up great clouds of perfume to the tree-tops.

'Peep!' said the field-mice when they awoke. They said it very softly. But since it was still grey dawn they said nothing else for a while. For a time it was perfectly still. Then a crow's hoarse rasping caw sounded far above in the sky. The crows had awakened and were visiting one another in the tree-tops. The magpie answered at once, 'Shackarakshak! Did you think I was still asleep?' Then a hundred small voices started in very softly here and there. Peep! peep! tiu! Sleep and the dark were still in these sounds. And they came from far apart.

Suddenly a blackbird flew to the top of a beech. She perched way up on the topmost twig that stuck up thin against the sky and sat there watching how, far away over the trees, the night-weary, pale-grey heavens were glowing in the distant east and coming to life. Then she commenced to sing.

Her little black body seemed only a tiny dark speck at that distance. She looked like a dead leaf. But she poured out her song in a great flood of rejoicing through the whole forest. And everything began to stir. The finches warbled, the little redthroat and the goldfinch were heard. The doves rushed from place to place with a loud clapping and rustling of wings. The pheasants cackled as though their throats would burst. The noise of their wings, as they flew from their roosts to the ground, was soft but powerful. They kept uttering their metallic splintering call with its soft ensuing chuckle. Far above, the falcons cried sharply and joyously, 'Yayaya!'

The sun rose.

'Diu diyu!' the yellow bird rejoiced. He flew to and fro among the branches, and his round yellow body flashed in the morning light like a winged ball of gold.

Bambi walked under the great oak on the meadow. It sparkled with dew. It smelled of grass and flowers and moist earth, and whispered of a thousand living things. Friend Hare was there and seemed to be thinking over something important. A haughty pheasant strutted slowly by, nibbling at the grass seeds and peering cautiously in all directions. The dark metallic blue on his neck gleamed in the sun.

One of the Princes was standing close to Bambi. Bambi had never seen any of the fathers so close before. The stag was standing right in front of him next to the hazel bush and was somewhat hidden by the branches. Bambi did not move. He wanted the Prince to come out completely and was wondering whether he dared speak to him. He wanted to ask his mother and looked around for her. But his mother had already gone away and was standing some distance off, beside Aunt Ena. At the same time Gobo and Faline came running out of the woods. Bambi was still thinking it over without stirring. If he went up to his mother and the others now he would have to pass by the Prince. He felt as if he couldn't do it.

'O well,' he thought, 'I don't have to ask my mother first. The old Prince spoke to me and I didn't tell mother anything about it. I'll say, "Good-morning, Prince." He can't be offended at that. But if he does get angry I'll run away fast.' Bambi struggled with his resolve which began to waver again.

Presently the Prince walked out from behind the hazel bush on to the meadow.

'Now,' thought Bambi.

Then there was a crash like thunder.

Bambi shrank together and didn't know what had happened. He saw the Prince leap into the air under his very nose and watched him rush past him into the forest with one great bound.

Bambi looked around in a daze. The thunder still vibrated. He saw how his mother and Aunt Ena, Gobo and Faline fled into the woods. He saw how Friend Hare scurried away like mad. He saw the pheasant running with his neck outstretched. He noticed that the forest grew suddenly still. He started and sprang into the thicket. He had made only a few bounds when he saw the Prince lying on the ground in front of him, motionless. Bambi stopped horrified,

not understanding what it meant. The Prince lay bleeding from a great wound in his shoulder. He was dead.

'Don't stop!' a voice beside commanded. It was his mother who rushed past at full gallop. 'Run,' she cried. 'Run as fast as you can!' She did not slow up, but raced ahead, and her command brought Bambi after her. He ran with all his might.

'What is it, Mother?' he asked. 'What is it, Mother?'

His mother answered between gasps, 'It – was – He!'

Bambi shuddered and they ran on. At last they stopped for lack of breath.

'What did you say? Tell me what it was you said?' a soft voice called down from overhead. Bambi looked up. The squirrel came chattering through the branches.

'I ran the whole way with you,' he cried. 'It was dreadful.'

'Were you there?' asked the mother.

'Of course I was there,' the squirrel replied. 'I am still trembling in every limb.' He sat erect, balancing with his splendid tail, displaying his small white chest, and holding his forepaws protestingly against his body. 'I'm beside myself with excitement,' he said.

'I'm quite weak from fright myself,' said the

mother. 'I don't understand it. Not one of us saw a thing.'

'Is that so?' the squirrel said pettishly. 'I saw Him long before.'

'So did I,' another voice cried. It was the magpie. She flew past and settled on a branch.

'So did I,' came a croak from above. It was the jay who was sitting on an ash.

A couple of crows in the tree-tops cawed harshly, 'We saw Him, too.'

They all sat around talking importantly. They were unusually excited and seemed to be full of anger and fear.

'Whom?' Bambi thought. 'Whom did they see?'

'I tried my best,' the squirrel was saying, pressing his forepaws protestingly against his heart. 'I tried my best to warn the poor Prince.'

'And I,' the jay rasped. 'How often did I scream? But he didn't care to hear me.'

'He didn't hear me either,' the magpie croaked. 'I called him at least ten times. I wanted to fly right past him, for, thought I, he hasn't heard me yet; I'll fly to the hazel bush where he's standing. He can't help hearing me there. But at that minute it happened.'

'My voice is probably louder than yours, and I warned him as well as I could,' the crow said in an impudent tone. 'But gentlemen of that stamp pay little attention to the likes of us.'

'Much too little, really,' the squirrel agreed.

'Well, we did what we could,' said the magpie. 'We're certainly not to blame when an accident happens.'

'Such a handsome Prince,' the squirrel lamented. 'And in the very prime of life.'

'Akh!' croaked the jay. 'It would have been better for him if he hadn't been so proud and had paid more attention to us.'

'He certainly wasn't proud.'

'No more so than the other Princes of his family,' the magpie put in.

'Just plain stupid,' sneered the jay.

'You're stupid yourself,' the crow cried down from overhead. 'Don't you talk about stupidity. The whole forest knows how stupid you are.'

'I!' replied the jay, stiff with astonishment. 'Nobody can accuse me of being stupid. I may be forgetful but I'm certainly not stupid.'

'O just as you please,' said the crow solemnly. 'Forget what I said to you but remember that the Prince did not die because he was proud or stupid, but because no one can escape Him.'

'Akh!' croaked the jay. 'I don't like that kind of talk.' He flew away.

The crow went on, 'He has already outwitted many of my family. He kills what He wants. Nothing can help us.'

'You have to be on your guard against Him,' the magpie broke in.

'You certainly do,' said the crow sadly. 'Goodbye.' He flew off, with his family accompanying him.

Bambi looked around. His mother was no longer there.

'What are they talking about now?' thought Bambi. 'I can't understand what they are talking about. Who is this "He" they talk about? That was He, too, that I saw in the bushes, but He didn't kill me.'

Bambi thought of the Prince lying in front of him with his bloody mangled shoulder. He was dead now. Bambi walked along. The forest sang again with a thousand voices, the sun pierced the tree-tops with its broad rays. There was light everywhere. The leaves began to smell. Far above the falcons called, close at hand a woodpecker hammered as if nothing had happened. Bambi was not happy. He felt himself threatened by something dark. He did not understand how the others could be so carefree and happy while life was so difficult and dangerous. Then the desire seized him to go deeper and deeper into the woods. They lured him into their depths. He wanted to find some hiding place where, shielded on all sides by impenetrable thickets, he could never be seen. He never wanted to go to the meadows again.

Something moved very softly in the bushes. Bambi drew back violently. The old stag was standing in front of him.

Bambi trembled. He wanted to run away, but he controlled himself and remained. The old stag looked at him with his great deep eyes and asked. 'Were you out there before?'

'Yes,' Bambi said softly. His heart was pounding in his throat.

'Where is your mother?' asked the stag.

Bambi answered still very softly, 'I don't know.'

The old stag kept gazing at him. 'And still you're not calling for her?' he said.

Bambi looked into the noble, iron-grey face, looked at the stag's antlers and suddenly felt full of courage. 'I can stay by myself, too,' he said.

The old stag considered him for a while; then he asked gently, 'Aren't you the little one that was crying for his mother not long ago?'

Bambi was somewhat embarrassed, but his courage held. 'Yes, I am,' he confessed.

The old stag looked at him in silence and it seemed to Bambi as if those deep eyes gazed still more mildly. 'You scolded me then, Prince,' he cried excitedly, 'because I was afraid of being left alone. Since then I haven't been.'

The stag looked at Bambi appraisingly and smiled a very slight, hardly noticeable smile. Bambi noticed it, however. 'Noble Prince,' he asked confidently, 'what has happened? I don't understand it. Who is this "He" they are all talking about?' He stopped, terrified by the dark glance that bade him be silent.

Another pause ensued. The old stag was gazing past Bambi into the distance. Then he said slowly, 'Listen, smell and see for yourself. Find out for yourself.' He lifted his antlered head still higher. 'Farewell,' he said, nothing else. Then he vanished.

Bambi stood transfixed and wanted to cry. But that farewell still rang in his ears and sustained him. Farewell, the old stag had said, so he couldn't have been angry.

Bambi felt himself thrill with pride, felt inspired with a deep earnestness. Yes, life was difficult and full of danger. But come what might he would learn to bear it all.

He walked slowly deeper into the forest.

THE leaves were falling from the great oak at the meadow's edge. They were falling from all the trees.

One branch of the oak reached high above the others and stretched far out over the meadow. Two leaves clung to its very tip.

'It isn't the way it used to be,' said one leaf to the other.

'No,' the other leaf answered. 'So many of us have fallen off tonight, we're almost the only ones left on our branch.'

'You never know who's going to go next,' said the first leaf. 'Even when it was warm and the sun shone, a storm or a cloudburst would come sometimes, and many leaves were torn off, though they were still young. You never know who's going to go next.'

'The sun seldom shines now,' sighed the second leaf, 'and when it does it gives no warmth. We must have warmth again.'

'Can it be true,' said the first leaf, 'can it really be true, that others come to take our places when

83

we're gone and after them still others, and more and more?'

'It is really true,' whispered the second leaf. 'We can't even begin to imagine it, it's beyond our powers.'

'It makes me very sad,' added the first leaf.

They were silent a while. Then the first leaf said quietly to herself, 'Why must we fall . . .?'

The second leaf asked, 'What happens to us when we have fallen?'

'We sink down. . . .'

'What is under us?'

The first leaf answered, 'I don't know, some say one thing, some another, but nobody knows.'

The second leaf asked, 'Do we feel anything, do we know anything about ourselves when we're down there?'

The first leaf answered, 'Who knows? Not one of all those down there has ever come back to tell us about it.'

They were silent again. Then the first leaf said tenderly to the other, 'Don't worry so much about it, you're trembling.'

'That's nothing,' the second leaf answered, 'I tremble at the least thing now. I don't feel so sure of my hold as I used to.'

'Let's not talk any more about such things,' said the first leaf.

The other replied, 'No, we'll let be. But --

what else shall we talk about?' She was silent and went on after a little while, 'Which of us will go first?'

'There's still plenty of time to worry about that,' the other leaf assured her. 'Let's remember how beautiful it was, how wonderful, when the sun came out and shone so warmly that we thought we'd burst with life. Do you remember? And the morning dew, and the mild and splendid nights.. . .'

'Now the nights are dreadful,' the second leaf complained, 'and there is no end to them.'

'We shouldn't complain,' said the first leaf gently. 'We've outlived many, many others.'

'Have I changed much?' asked the second leaf shyly but determinedly.

'Not in the least,' the first leaf assured her. 'You only think so because I've got to be so yellow and ugly. But it's different in your case.'

'You're fooling me,' the second leaf said.

'No, really,' the first leaf exclaimed eagerly, 'believe me, you're as lovely as the day you were born. Here and there may be a little yellow spot, but it's hardly noticeable and only makes you handsomer, believe me.'

'Thanks,' whispered the second leaf, quite touched. 'I don't believe you, not altogether, but I thank you because you're so kind, you've always been so kind to me. I'm just beginning to understand how kind you are.'

'Hush,' said the other leaf, and kept silent herself, for she was too troubled to talk any more.

Then they were both silent. Hours passed.

A moist wind blew, cold and hostile, through the tree-tops.

'Ah, now,' said the second leaf, 'I . . .' Then her voice broke off. She was torn from her place and spun down.

Winter had come.

Bᴀᴍʙɪ noticed that the world was changed. It was hard for him to get used to this altered world. They had all lived like rich folk and now had fallen upon hard times. For Bambi knew nothing but abundance. He took it for granted that he would always have plenty to eat. He thought he would never need to trouble about food. He believed he would always sleep in the lovely green-leafed glade where no one could see him, and would always go about in his smooth, handsome, glossy red coat.

Now everything was changed without his having noticed the change take place. The process that was ending had seemed only a series of episodes to him. It pleased him to see the milk-white veils of mist steam from the meadow in the morning, or drop suddenly from the grey sky at dawn. They vanished so beautifully in the sunshine. The hoar-frost that covered the meadow with such dazzling whiteness delighted him, too. Sometimes he liked to listen to his big cousins, the elk. The whole forest would tremble with their kingly voices. Bambi used to listen and be very much frightened, but his heart would beat high with admiration when he heard them calling. He remembered that the kings had antlers branching like tall, strong trees. And it seemed to him that their voices were as powerful as their antlers. Whenever he heard the deep tones of those voices he would stand motionless. Their deep voices rolled towards him like the mighty moaning of noble, maddened blood whose primal power was giving utterance to longing, rage and pride. Bambi struggled in vain against his fears. They overpowered him whenever he heard those voices, but he was proud to have such noble relatives. At the same time he felt a strange sense of annoyance because they were so unapproachable. It offended and humiliated him without his knowing exactly how or why, even without his being particularly conscious of it.

It was only after the mating season had passed and the thunder of the stags' mighty voices had grown still, that Bambi began to notice other things once more. At night when he roamed through the forest or by day as he lay in the glade, he heard the falling leaves whisper among the trees. They fluttered and rustled ceaselessly through the air from all the tree-tops and branches. A delicate silvery sound was falling constantly to earth. It was wonderful to awaken amidst it, wonderful to fall asleep to this mysterious and melancholy whispering. Soon the leaves lay thick and loose on the ground and when you walked through them they flew about, softly rustling. It was jolly to push them aside with every step, they were piled so high. It made a sound like, 'Sh! Sh!', soft and very clear and silvery. Besides, it was very useful, for Bambi had to be particularly careful these days to hear and smell everything. And with the leaves you could hear everything far off. They rustled at the slightest touch and cried, 'Sh! Sh!' Nobody could steal through them.

But then the rain came. It poured down from early morning till late at night. Sometimes it rained all night long and into the following day. It would stop for a while and begin again with fresh strength. The air was damp and cold, the whole world seemed full of rain. If you tried to nibble a little meadow grass you got your mouth full of water, or if you tugged the least little bit at a bough a whole torrent of water poured into your eyes and nose. The leaves no longer rustled. They lay pale and soggy on the ground, flattened by the rain and made no sounds. Bambi discovered for the first time how unpleasant it is to be rained on all day and all night until you are soaked to the skin. There had not even been a frost yet, but he longed for the warm weather and felt it was a sad business to have to run around soaked through.

But when the north wind blew, Bambi found out what cold is. It wasn't much help to nestle close to his mother. Of course at first he thought it was wonderful to lie there and keep one side warm at least. But the north wind raged through the forest all day and all night long. It seemed to be driven to madness by some incomprehensible ice-cold fury, as though it wanted to tear up the forest by its roots or annihilate it somehow. The trees groaned in stubborn resistance, they struggled mightily against the wind's fierce on-slaught. You could hear their long-drawn moans, their sigh-like creakings, the loud snap when their strong limbs split, the angry crack-ing when now and again a trunk broke and the vanquished tree seemed to shriek from every wound in its rent and dying body. Nothing else could be heard, for the storm swooped down still more fiercely on the forest, and its roaring drowned all lesser noises.

Then Bambi knew that want and hardship had come. He saw how much the rain and wind had changed the world. There was no longer a leaf on tree or bush. But all stood there as though violated, their bodies naked for all to see. And they lifted their bare brown limbs to the sky for pity. The grass on the meadow was withered and shortened, as if it had sunk into the earth. Even the glade seemed wretched and bare. Since the leaves had fallen it was no longer possible to lie so well hidden as before. The glade was open on all sides.

One day, as a young magpie flew over the meadow, something cold and white fell in her eye. Then it fell again and again. She felt as if a little veil were drawn across her eye while the small, pale, blinding-white flakes danced around her. The magpie hesitated in her flight, fluttered a little, and then soared straight up into the air. In vain. The cold white flakes were everywhere and got into her eyes again. She kept flying straight up, soaring higher.

'Don't put yourself out so much, dearie,' a crow who was flying above her in the same direction called down, 'Don't put yourself out so much. You can't fly high enough to get outside these flakes. This is snow.'

'Snow!' cried the magpie in surprise, struggling against the drizzle.

'That's about the size of it,' said the crow. 'It's winter, and this is snow.'

'Excuse me,' the magpie replied, 'but I only

left the nest in May. I don't know anything about winter.'

'There are plenty in the same boat,' the crow remarked, 'but you'll soon find out.'

'Well,' said the magpie, 'if this is snow I think I'll sit down for a while.' She perched on an elder and shook herself. The crow flew awkwardly away.

At first Bambi was delighted with the snow. The air was calm and mild while the white snow-stars whirled down and the world looked completely different. It had grown lighter, gayer, Bambi thought, and whenever the sun came out for a little while everything shone and the white covering flashed and sparkled so brightly that it blinded you.

But Bambi soon stopped being pleased with the snow. For it grew harder and harder to find food. He had to paw the snow away with endless labour before he could find one withered little blade of grass. The snow-crust cut his legs and he was afraid of cutting his feet. Gobo had already cut his. Of course Gobo was the kind who couldn't stand anything and was a constant source of trouble to his mother.

The deer were always together now and were much more friendly than before. Ena brought her children constantly. Lately Marena, a half-grown doe, had joined the circle. But old Nettla really contributed most to their entertainment. She was quite a self-sufficient person and had her own ideas about everything. 'No,' she would say, 'I don't bother with children any more. I've had enough of that particular joke.'

Faline asked, 'What difference does it make, if they're a joke?' And Nettla would act as if she were angry, and say, 'They're a bad joke, though, and I've had enough of them.'

They got along perfectly together. They would sit side by side gossiping. The young ones had never had a chance to hear so much.

Even one or another of the Princes would join them now. At first things went somewhat stiffly, especially since the children were a little shy. But that soon changed, and they got along very well together. Bambi admired Prince Ronno, who was a stately lord, and he passionately loved the handsome young Karus. They had dropped their horns and Bambi often looked at the two slate-grey round spots that showed smooth and shimmering with many delicate points on the Prince's heads. They looked very noble.

It was terribly interesting whenever one of the Princes talked about Him. Ronno had a thick hide-covered swelling on his left forefoot. He limped on that foot and used to ask sometimes, 'Can you really see that I limp?' Everyone would hasten to assure him that there was not the trace of a limp. That was what Ronno wanted. And it really was hardly noticeable.

'Yes,' he would go on. 'I saved myself from a tight corner that time.' And then Ronno would tell how He had surprised him and hurled his fire at him. But it had only struck his leg. It had driven him nearly mad with pain, and no wonder, since the bone was shattered. But Ronno did not lose his head. He was up and away on three legs. He pressed on in spite of his weakness, for he saw that he was being pursued. He ran without stopping until night came. Then he gave himself a rest. But he went on the next morning until he felt he was in safety. Then he took care of himself, living alone in hiding, waiting for his wound to heal. At last he came out again and was a hero. He limped, but he thought no one noticed it.

They were often together now for long periods and told many stories. Bambi heard more about Him than ever before. They told how terrible He was to look at. No one could bear to look at His pale face. Bambi knew that already from his own experience. They spoke too about His smell, and again Bambi could have spoken if he had not been too well brought up to mix in his elders' conversation. They said that His smell differed each time in a hundred subtle ways and yet you could tell it in an instant, for it was always exciting, unfathomable, mysterious and terrible.

They told how He used only two legs to walk with and they spoke of the amazing strength of His two hands. Some of them did not know what hands were. But when it was explained, old Nettla said, 'I don't see anything so surprising in that. A squirrel can do everything you tell about just as well, and every little mouse can perform the same wonders.' She turned away her head disdainfully.

'O no,' cried the others, and they gave her to understand that those were *not* the same things at all. But old Nettla was not to be cowed. 'What about the falcon?' she exclaimed. 'And the buzzard? And the owl? They've got only two legs and when they want to catch something they simply stand on one leg and grab with the other. That's much harder and He certainly can't do that.'

Old Nettla was not at all inclined to admire anything connected with Him. She hated Him with all her heart. 'He is loathsome,' she said, and she stuck to that. Besides, nobody contradicted her, since nobody liked Him.

But the talk grew more complicated when they told how He had a third hand, not two hands merely, but a third hand.

'That's an old story,' Nettla said curtly. 'I don't believe it.'

'Is that so?' Ronno broke in. 'Then what did he shatter my leg with? Can you tell me that?'

Old Nettla answered carelessly, 'That's your affair my dear, He's never shattered any of mine.'

Aunt Ena said, 'I've seen a good deal in my time, and I think there's something in the story that He has a third hand.'

'I agree with you,' young Karus said politely. 'I have a friend, a crow . . .' He paused, embarrassed for a moment, and looked around at them, one after the other, as though he were afraid of being laughed at. But when he saw that they were listening attentively to him he went on. 'This crow is unusually well informed, I must say that. Surprisingly well informed. And she says that He really has three hands, but not always. The third hand is the bad one, the crow says. It isn't attached like the other two, but he carries it hanging over His shoulder. The crow says that she can always tell exactly when He, or anyone like Him, is going to be dangerous. If He comes without the third hand He isn't dangerous.'

Old Nettla laughed. 'Your crow's a blockhead, my dear Karus,' she said. 'Tell her so for me. If she were as clever as she thinks she is,

she'd know that He's always dangerous, always.'
But the others had different objections.

Bambi's mother said, 'Some of Them aren't dangerous; you can see that at a glance.'

'Is that so?' old Nettla asked. 'I suppose you stand still till They come up to you and wish you a good day.'

Bambi's mother answered gently, 'Of course I don't stand still; I run away.'

And Faline broke in with, 'You should always run away.' Everybody laughed.

But when they talked about the third hand they became serious and fear grew on them gradually. For whatever it might be, a third hand or something else, it was terrible and they did not understand it. They only knew of it from others' stories, few of them had ever seen it for themselves. He would stand still, far off, and never move. You couldn't explain what He did or how it happened, but suddenly there would be a crash like thunder, fire would shoot out and far away from Him you would drop down dying with your breast torn open. They all sat bowed while they talked about Him, as though they felt the presence of some dark, unknown power controlling them.

They listened curiously to the many stories that were always horrible, full of blood and suffering. They listened tirelessly to everything

97

that was said about Him, tales that were certainly invented, all the stories and sayings that had come down from their fathers and great-grandfathers. In each one of them they were unconsciously seeking for some way to propitiate this dark power, or some way to escape it.

'What difference does it make,' young Karus asked quite despondently, 'how far away He is when He kills you?'

'Didn't your clever crow explain that to you?' old Nettla mocked.

'No,' said Karus with a smile. 'She says that she's often seen Him but no one can explain Him.'

'Yes, he knocks the crows out of the trees, too, when he wants to,' Ronno observed.

'And he brings down the pheasant on the wing,' Aunt Ena added.

Bambi's mother said, 'He throws his hand at you, my grandmother told me so.'

'Is that so?' asked old Nettla. 'What is it that bangs so terribly then?'

'That's when he tears his hand off,' Bambi's mother explained. 'Then the fire flashes and the thunder cracks. He's all fire inside.'

'Excuse me,' said Ronno. 'It's true that He's all fire inside. But that about His hand is wrong. A hand couldn't make such wounds. You can see that for yourself. It's much more likely that it's a tooth He throws at us. A tooth would explain a great many things, you know. You really die from his bite.'

'Will he never stop hunting us?' young Karus sighed.

Then Marena spoke, the young half-grown doe. 'They say that some time He'll come to live with us and be as gentle as we are. He'll play with us then and the whole forest will be happy, and we'll be friends with Him.'

Old Nettla burst out laughing. 'Let Him stay where He is and leave us in peace,' she said.

Aunt Ena said reprovingly, 'You shouldn't talk that way.'

'And why not?' old Nettla replied hotly. 'I really don't see why not. Friends with Him! He's murdered us ever since we can remember, everyone of us, our sisters, our mothers, our brothers! Ever since we came into the world He's given us no peace, but has killed us wherever we showed our heads. And now we're going to be friends with Him! What nonsense!'

Marena looked at all of them out of her big, calm, shining eyes. 'Love is no nonsense,' she said. 'It has to come.'

Old Nettla turned away. 'I'm going to look for something to eat,' she said, and trotted off.

WINTER dragged on. Sometimes it was warmer, but then the snow would fall again and lie deeper and deeper, so that it became impossible to scrape it away. It was worst when the thaws came and the melted snow water froze again in the night. Then there was a thin slippery film of ice. Often it broke in pieces and the sharp splinters cut the deer's tender fetlocks till they bled.

A heavy frost had set in several days before. The air was purer and rarer than it had ever been, and full of energy. It began to hum in a very fine high tone. It hummed with the cold.

It was silent in the woods, but something horrible happened every day. Once the crows fell upon Friend Hare's small son who was lying sick, and killed him in a cruel way. He could be heard moaning pitifully for a long while. Friend Hare was not at home, and when he heard the sad news he was beside himself with grief.

Another time the squirrel raced about with a great wound in his neck where the ferret had caught him. By a miracle the squirrel had escaped. He could not talk because of the pain, but he ran up and down the branches. Everyone could see him. He ran like mad. From time to time he stopped, sat down, raised his forepaws desperately and clutched his head in terror and agony while the red blood oozed on his white chest. He ran about for an hour, then suddenly crumpled up, fell across a branch, and dropped dead in the snow. A couple of magpies flew down at once to begin their meal.

Another day a fox tore to pieces the strong and handsome pheasant who had enjoyed such general respect and popularity. His death aroused the sympathies of a wide circle who tried to comfort his disconsolate widow.

The fox had dragged the pheasant out of the snow, where he was buried, thinking himself well hidden. No one could have felt safer than the pheasant, for it all happened in broad daylight. The terrible hardship that seemed to have no end spread bitterness and brutality. It destroyed all their memories of the past, their faith in each other, and ruined every good custom they had. There was no longer either peace or mercy in the forest.

'It's hard to believe that it will ever be better,' Bambi's mother sighed.

Aunt Ena sighed too. 'It's hard to believe that

it was ever any better,' she said.

'And yet,' Marena said, looking in front of her, 'I always think how beautiful it was before.'

'Look,' old Nettla said to Aunt Ena, 'your little one is trembling.' She pointed to Gobo. 'Does he always tremble like that?'

'Yes,' Aunt Ena answered gravely, 'he's shivered that way for the last few days.'

'Well,' said old Nettla in her frank way, 'I'm glad that I have no more children. If that little one were mine I'd wonder if he'd last out the winter.'

The future really didn't look very bright for Gobo. He was weak. He had always been much more delicate than Bambi or Faline and remained smaller than either of them. He was growing worse from day to day. He could not eat even the little food there was. It made his stomach ache. And he was quite exhausted by the cold, and by the horrors around him. He shivered more and more and could hardly stand up. Everyone looked at him sympathetically.

Old Nettla went up to him and nudged him good-naturedly. 'Don't be so sad,' she said encouragingly, 'that's no way for a little prince to act, and besides it's unhealthy.' She turned away so that no one should see how moved she was.

Ronno, who had settled himself a little to one side in the snow, suddenly sprang up. 'I don't know what it is,' he mumbled and gazed around.

Everyone grew watchful. 'What is it?' they asked.

'I don't know,' Ronno repeated. 'But I'm restless. I suddenly felt restless as if something were wrong.'

Karus was snuffing the air. 'I don't smell anything strange,' he declared.

They all stood still, listening and snuffing the air. 'It's nothing, there's absolutely nothing to smell,' they agreed one after another.

'Nevertheless,' Ronno insisted, 'you can say what you like, something is wrong.'

Marena said, 'The crows are calling.'

'There they go calling again,' Faline added quickly, but the others had already heard them.

'They are flying,' said Karus and the others.

Everybody looked up. High above the treetops a flock of crows flapped by. They came from the farthest edge of the forest, the direction from which danger always came, and they were complaining to one another. Apparently something unusual had happened.

'Wasn't I right,' asked Ronno. 'You can see that something is happening.'

'What shall we do?' Bambi's mother whispered anxiously.

'Let's get away,' Aunt Ena urged in alarm.

'Wait,' Ronno commanded.

'But the children,' Aunt Ena replied, 'the children. Gobo can't run.'

'Go ahead,' Ronno agreed, 'go off with your children. I don't think there's any need for it, but I don't blame you for going.' He was alert and serious.

'Come, Gobo. Come, Faline. Softly now, go slowly. And keep behind me,' Aunt Ena warned them. She slipped away with the children.

Time passed. They stood still, listening and trembling.

'As if we hadn't suffered enough already,' old Nettla began. 'We still have this to go through . . .' She was very angry. Bambi looked at her, and he felt that she was thinking of something horrible.

Three or four magpies had already begun to chatter on the side of the thicket from which the crows had come. 'Look out! look out, out, out!' they cried. The deer could not see them, but could hear them calling and warning each other. Sometimes one of them, and sometimes all of them together, would cry, 'Look out, out, out!' Then they came nearer. They fluttered in terror from tree to tree, peered back and fluttered away again in fear and alarm.

'Akh!' cried the jays. They screamed their warning loudly.

Suddenly all the deer shrank together at once

as though a blow had struck them. Then they stood still snuffing the air.

It was He.

A heavy wave of scent blew past. There was nothing they could do. The scent filled their nostrils, it numbed their senses and made their hearts stop beating.

The magpies were still chattering. The jays were still screaming overhead. In the woods around them everything had sprung to life. The field-mice flitted through the branches, like tiny feathered balls, chirping, 'Run! run!'

The blackbirds fled swiftly and darkly above them with long-drawn twittering cries. Through the dark tangle of bare bushes, they saw on the white snow a wild aimless scurrying of smaller, shadowy creatures. These were the pheasants. Then a flash of red streaked by. That was the fox. But no one was afraid of him now. For that fearful scent kept streaming on in a wider wave, sending terror into their hearts and uniting them all in one mad fear, in a single feverish impulse to flee, to save themselves.

That mysterious overpowering scent filled the woods with such strength that they knew that this time He was not alone, but had come with many others, and there would be no end to the killing.

They did not move. They looked at the field-mice, whisking away in a sudden flutter, at the blackbirds and the squirrels who dashed from tree-top to tree-top in mad bounds. They knew that all the little creatures on the ground had nothing to fear. But they understood their flight when they smelt Him, for no forest creature could bear his presence.

Presently Friend Hare hopped up. He hesitated, sat still and then hopped on again.

'What is it?' Karus called after him impatiently.

But Friend Hare only looked around with bewildered eyes and could not even speak. He was completely terrified.

'What's the use of asking?' said Ronno gloomily.

Friend Hare gasped for breath. 'We are surrounded,' he said in a lifeless voice. 'We can't escape on any side. He is everywhere.'

At the same instant they heard His voice. Twenty or thirty strong, He cried, 'Ho! Ho! Ha! Ha!' It roared like the sound of winds and storms. He beat on the tree trunks as though they were drums. It was racking and terrifying. A distant twisting and rending of parted bushes rang out. There was a snapping and cracking of broken boughs.

He was coming.

He was coming into the heart of the thicket.

Then short whistling flute-like trills sounded together with the loud flap of soaring wings. A pheasant rose from under His very feet. The deer heard the wing-beats of the pheasant grow fainter as he mounted into the air. There was a loud crash like thunder. Then silence. Then a dull thud on the ground.

'He is dead,' said Bambi's mother, trembling. 'The first,' Ronno added.

The young doe, Marena, said, 'In this very hour many of us are going to die. Perhaps I shall be one of them.' No one listened to her, for a mad terror had seized them all.

Bambi tried to think. But His savage noises grew louder and louder and paralysed Bambi's senses. He heard nothing but those noises. They numbed him while amidst the howling, shouting and crashing he could hear his own heart pounding. He felt nothing but curiosity and did not even realize that he was trembling in every limb. From time to time his mother whispered in his ear, 'Stay close to me.' She was shouting, but in the uproar it sounded to Bambi as if she were whispering. Her 'Stay close to me' encouraged him. It was like a chain holding him. Without it he would have rushed off senselessly, and he heard it at the very moment when his wits were wandering and he wanted to dash away.

He looked around. All sorts of creatures were swarming past, scampering blindly over one another. A pair of weasels ran by like thin snake-like streaks. The eye could scarcely follow them. A ferret listened as though bewitched to every shriek that desperate Friend Hare let out.

A fox was standing in a whole flurry of fluttering pheasants. They paid no attention to him. They ran right under his nose and he paid no attention to them. Motionless, with his head thrust forward, he listened to the onrushing tumult, lifting his pointed ears and snuffing the air with his nose. Only his tail moved, slowly wagging with his intense concentration.

A pheasant dashed up. He had come from where the danger was worst, and was beside himself with fear.

'Don't try to fly,' he shouted to the others. 'Don't fly, just run! Don't lose your head! Don't try to fly! Just run, run, run!'

He kept repeating the same thing over and over again as though to encourage himself. But he no longer knew what he was saying.

'Ho! ho! ha! ha!' came the death cry from quite near apparently.

'Don't lose your head,' screamed the pheasant. And at the same time his voice broke in a whistling gasp and, spreading his wings, he flew up with a loud whir. Bambi watched how he

flew straight up, directly between the trees, beating his wings. The dark metallic blue and greenish-brown markings on his body gleamed like gold. His long tail feathers swept proudly behind him. A short crash like thunder sounded sharply. The pheasant suddenly crumpled up in mid-flight. He turned head over tail as though he wanted to catch his claws with his beak, and then dropped violently to earth. He fell among the others and did not move again.

Then everyone lost his senses. They all rushed towards one another. Five or six pheasants rose at one time with a loud whir. 'Don't fly,' cried the rest, and ran. The thunder cracked five or six times and more of the flying birds dropped lifeless to the ground.

'Come,' said Bambi's mother. Bambi looked around. Ronno and Karus had already fled. Old Nettla was disappearing. Only Marena was still beside them. Bambi went with his mother, Marena following them timidly. All around them was a roaring and shouting, and the thunder was crashing. Bambi's mother was calm. She trembled quietly but she kept her wits together.

'Bambi, my child,' she said, 'keep behind me all the time. We'll have to get out of here and across the open place. But now we'll go slowly.'

The din was maddening. The thunder crashed ten, twelve times as He hurled it from his hands.

'Look out,' said Bambi's mother. 'Don't run. But when we have to cross the open place, run as fast as you can. And don't forget, Bambi my child, don't pay any attention to me when we get out there. Even if I fall, don't pay any attention to me, just keep on running. Do you understand, Bambi?'

His mother walked carefully step by step amidst the uproar. The pheasants were running up and down, burying themselves in the snow. Suddenly they would spring out and begin to run again. The whole Hare family was hopping to and fro, squatting down and then hopping again. No one said a word. They were all spent with terror and numbed by the din and the thunderclaps.

It grew lighter in front of Bambi and his mother. The clearing showed through the bushes. Behind them the terrifying drumming on the tree trunks came crashing nearer and nearer. The breaking branches snapped. There was a roaring of 'Ha! ha! ho! ho!'

Then Friend Hare and two of his cousins rushed past them across the clearing. Bing! Ping! Bang! roared the thunder. Bambi saw how Friend Hare struck an elder in the middle of his flight and lay with his white belly turned upward. He quivered a little and then was still. Bambi stood petrified. But from behind him came the cry, 'Here they are! Run! Run!'

There was a loud clapping of wings suddenly opened. There were gasps, sobs, showers of feathers, flutterings. The pheasants took wing and the whole flock rose almost at one instant. The air was throbbing with repeated thunder claps and the dull thuds of the fallen and the high piercing shrieks of those who had escaped.

Bambi heard steps and looked behind him. He was there. He came bursting through the bushes on all sides. He sprang up everywhere, struck about Him, beat the bushes, drummed on the tree trunks and shouted with a fiendish voice.

'Now,' said Bambi's mother. 'Get away from here. And don't stay too close to me.' She was off with a bound that barely skimmed the snow. Bambi rushed out after her. The thunder crashed around them on all sides. It seemed as if the earth would split in half. Bambi saw nothing. He kept running. A growing desire to get away from the tumult and out of reach of that scent which seemed to strangle him, the growing impulse to flee, the longing to save himself were loosed in him at last. He ran. It seemed to him as if he saw his mother hit but he did not know if it was really she or not. He felt a film come over his eyes from fear of the thunder crashing behind him. It had gripped him completely at last. He could think of nothing or see nothing around him. He kept running.

The open space was crossed. Another thicket took him in. The hue and cry still rang behind him. The sharp reports still thundered. And in the branches above him there was a light pattering like the first fall of hail. Then it grew quieter. Bambi kept running.

A dying pheasant with its neck twisted lay on the snow, beating feebly with its wings. When he heard Bambi coming he ceased his convulsive movements and whispered, 'It's all over with me.' Bambi paid no attention to him and ran on.

A tangle of bushes he blundered into forced him to slacken his pace and look for a path. He pawed the ground impatiently with his hoofs. 'This way,' called someone with a gasping voice. Bambi obeyed involuntarily and found an opening at once. Someone moved feebly in front of him. It was Friend Hare's wife who had called.

'Can you help me a little?' she said. Bambi looked at her and shuddered. Her hind leg dangled lifelessly in the snow, dyeing it red and melting it with warm oozing blood. 'Can you help me a little?' she repeated. She spoke as if she were well and whole, almost as if she were happy. 'I don't know what can have happened to me,' she went on. 'There's really no sense to it, but I just can't seem to walk....'

In the middle of her words she rolled over on her side and died. Bambi was seized with horror again and ran.

'Bambi!'

He stopped with a jolt. A deer was calling him. Again he heard the cry. 'Is that you, Bambi?'

Bambi saw Gobo floundering helplessly in the

snow. All his strength was gone; he could no
longer stand on his feet. He lay there half buried
and lifted his head feebly. Bambi went up to
him excitedly.

'Where's your mother, Gobo?' he asked, gasping for breath. 'Where's Faline?' Bambi spoke
quickly and impatiently. Terror still gripped
his heart.

'Mother and Faline had to go on,' Gobo
answered resignedly. He spoke softly, but as
seriously and as well as a grown deer. 'They had
to leave me here. I fell down. You must go on,
too, Bambi.'

'Get up,' cried Bambi. 'Get up, Gobo! You've
rested long enough. There's not a minute to lose
now. Get up and come with me!'

'No, leave me,' Gobo answered quietly, 'I
can't stand up. It's impossible. I'd like to, but
I'm too weak.'

'What will happen to you?' Bambi persisted.

'I don't know. Probably I'll die,' said Gobo
simply.

The uproar began again and re-echoed. New
crashes of thunder followed. Bambi shrank together. Suddenly a branch snapped. Young
Karus pounded swiftly through the snow, galloping ahead of the din.

'Run,' he called when he saw Bambi. 'Don't
stand there if you can run!' He was gone in a

flash and his headlong flight carried Bambi along with it. Bambi was hardly aware that he had begun to run again, and only after an interval did he say, 'Good-bye, Gobo.' But he was already too far away. Gobo could no longer hear him.

He ran till night-fall through the woods that were filled with shouting and thunder. As darkness closed in, it grew quiet. Soon a light wind carried away the horrible scent that spread everywhere. But the excitement remained.

The first friend whom Bambi saw again was Ronno. He was limping more than ever.

'Over in the oak grove the fox has a burning fever from his wound,' Ronno said. 'I just passed him. He's suffering terribly. He keeps biting the snow and the ground.'

'Have you seen my mother?' asked Bambi.

'No,' answered Ronno evasively, and walked quickly away.

Later during the night Bambi met old Nettla with Faline. All three were delighted to meet.

'Have you seen my mother?' asked Bambi.

'No,' Faline answered. 'I don't even know where my own mother is.'

'Well,' said old Nettla cheerfully, 'here's a nice mess. I was so glad that I didn't have to bother with children any more and now I have to look after two at once. I'm heartily grateful.'

Bambi and Faline laughed.

They talked about Gobo. Bambi told how he had found him, and they grew so sad they began to cry. But old Nettla would not have them crying. 'Before everything else you have got to get something to eat. I never heard of such a thing. You haven't had a bite to eat this livelong day!'

She led them to places where there were still a few leaves that had not completely withered. Old Nettla was wonderfully gentle. She ate nothing herself, but made Bambi and Faline eat heartily. She pawed away the snow from the grassy spots and ordered them to eat with, 'The grass is good here.' Or else she would say, 'No, wait. We'll find something better farther on.' But between whiles she would grumble. 'It's perfectly ridiculous the trouble children give you.'

Suddenly they saw Aunt Ena coming and rushed towards her. 'Aunt Ena,' cried Bambi. He had seen her first. Faline was beside herself with joy and bounded around her. 'Mother,' she cried. But Ena was weeping and nearly dead from exhaustion.

'Gobo is gone,' she cried. 'I've looked for him. I went to the little place where he lay when he broke down in the snow ... there was nothing there ... he is gone ... my poor little Gobo ...'

Old Nettla grumbled, 'If you had looked for

his tracks it would have been more sensible than crying,' she said.

'There weren't any tracks,' said Aunt Ena. 'But ... His ... tracks were there. He found Gobo.'

She was silent. Then Bambi asked despondently, 'Aunt Ena, have you seen my mother?'

'No,' answered Aunt Ena gently.

Bambi never saw his mother again.

A T last the willows shed their catkins. Everything was turning green, but the young leaves on the trees and bushes were still tiny. Glowing with the soft early morning light they looked fresh and smiling like children who have just awakened from sleep.

Bambi was standing in front of a hazel bush, beating his new antlers against the wood. It was very pleasant to do that. And an absolute necessity, besides, since skin and hide still covered his splendid antlers. The skin had to come off, of course, and no sensible creature would ever wait until it split of its own accord. Bambi pounded his antlers till the skin split and long strips of it dangled about his ears. As he pounded on the hazel stems again and again, he felt how much stronger his antlers were than the wood. This feeling shot through him in a rush of power and pride. He beat more fiercely on the hazel bush and tore its bark into long pieces. The white body of the tree showed naked and quickly turned a rusty red in the open air. But Bambi paid no attention to that. He saw the bright wood of the tree flash under his strokes and it heartened him. A whole row of hazel bushes bore traces of his work.

'Well, you are nearly grown now,' said a cheerful voice close by.

Bambi tossed his head and looked around him. There sat the squirrel observing him in a friendly way. From overhead came a short shrill laugh, 'Ha! Ha!'

Bambi and the squirrel were both half frightened. But the woodpecker, who was clinging to an oak-trunk, called down, 'Excuse me, but I always have to laugh when I see you deer acting like that.'

'What is there to laugh at?' asked Bambi politely.

'O!' said the woodpecker, 'you go at things in such a wrong-headed way. In the first place you ought to try big trees, for you can't get anything out of those little wisps of hazel stalks.'

'What should I get out of them?' Bambi asked.

'Insects,' said the woodpecker with a laugh. 'Insects and grubs. Look, do like this.' He drummed on the oak trunk, tack! tack! tack! tack!

The squirrel rushed up and scolded him. 'What are you talking about?' he said. 'The Prince isn't looking for insects and grubs.'

'Why not?' said the woodpecker, in high glee. 'They are lovely.' He bit an insect in half, swallowed it, and began drumming again.

'You don't understand,' the squirrel went on scolding. 'A noble lord like that has far other, far higher aims. You're only casting reflection on yourself by such talk.'

'It's all the same to me,' answered the woodpecker. 'A fig for higher aims,' he cried cheerfully, and fluttered away. The squirrel bustled down again.

'Don't you remember me?' he said, putting on a pleased expression.

'Very well,' answered Bambi in a friendly way. 'Do you live up there?' he asked, pointing to the oak.

The squirrel looked at him good-humouredly. 'You're mixing me up with my grandmother,' he said. 'I knew you were mixing me up with her. My grandmother used to live up there when you were just a baby, Prince Bambi. She often told me about you. The ferret killed her long ago, last winter, you may remember it.'

'Yes,' Bambi nodded. 'I have heard about it.'

'Well, afterwards my father settled here,' the squirrel went on. He sat erect and held both forepaws politely over his white chest. 'But maybe you've got me mixed up with my father, too. Did you know my father?'

'I'm sorry,' Bambi replied. 'But I never had that pleasure.'

'I thought so,' the squirrel exclaimed, satisfied. 'Father was so surly and so shy. He had nothing to do with anybody.'

'Where is he now?' Bambi inquired.

'Oh,' said the squirrel, 'the owl caught him a month ago. Yes. . . . And now I'm living up there myself. I'm quite content, since I was born up there.'

Bambi turned to go.

'Wait,' cried the squirrel quickly. 'I didn't mean to talk about all that. I wanted to say something quite different.'

Bambi stopped. 'What is it?' he asked patiently.

'Yes,' said the squirrel, 'what is it?' He thought a little while and then gave a quick skip and sat erect, balancing with his splendid tail. He looked at Bambi. 'Right you are,' he chattered on. 'Now I know what it was. I wanted to say that your antlers are almost grown now, and that you are going to be a remarkably handsome person.'

'Do you really think so?' said Bambi joyfully.

'Remarkably handsome,' cried the squirrel, and pressed his forepaws rapturously against his white chest. 'So tall, so stately and with such long bright prongs to your antlers. You don't often see the like.'

'Really?' Bambi asked. He was so delighted that he immediately began to beat the hazel stems again. He tore off long ribbons of bark.

All the while the squirrel kept on talking. 'I must say that very few have antlers like those at your age. It doesn't seem possible. I saw you several times from a distance last summer, and

I can hardly believe that you're the same creature, you were such a thin little shaver then.'

Bambi suddenly grew silent. 'Good-bye,' he said hastily, 'I have to go now.' And he ran off.

He didn't like to be reminded of last summer. He had had a difficult time of it since then. At first, after his mother's disappearance, he had felt quite lost. The long winter was interminable. Spring came hesitatingly and it was late before things began to turn green. Without old Nettla Bambi might not even have pulled through at all, but she looked after him and helped him where she could. In spite of that he was alone a good deal.

He missed Gobo at every turn; poor Gobo, who was dead too, like the rest of them. Bambi thought of him often during that winter, and for the first time he really began to appreciate how good and lovable Gobo had been.

He seldom saw Faline. She stayed with her mother most of the time, and seemed to have grown unusually shy. Later, when it had finally grown warm, Bambi began to feel his old self once more. He flourished his first antler on high and was very proud of it. But bitter disappointment soon followed.

The other bucks chased him whenever they saw him. They drove him away angrily. They would not let him come near them until finally

he was afraid to take a step for fear of being caught. He was afraid to show himself anywhere and slunk along hidden trails in a very downcast frame of mind.

As the summer days grew warmer a remarkable restlessness seized him. His heart felt more and more oppressed with a sense of longing that was both pleasant and painful. Whenever he chanced to see Faline or one of her friends, though only at a distance, a rush of incomprehensible excitement crept over him. Often it happened that he recognized her track or the air he snuffed told him she was near. Then he would feel himself irresistibly drawn towards her. But when he gave way to his desire he always came to grief. Either he met no one and, after wandering around for a long while, had to admit that they were avoiding him, or he ran across one of the bucks who immediately sprang

at him, beat and kicked him and chased him disgracefully away. Ronno and Karus had treated him worst of all. No, that hadn't been a happy time.

And now the squirrel had stupidly reminded him of it. Suddenly he became quite wild and started to run. The field-mice and hedge-sparrows flitted, frightened, through the bushes as he passed, and asked each other in a fluster, 'What was that?' Bambi did not hear them. A couple of magpies chattered nervously, 'What happened?' The jay cried angrily, 'What is the matter with you?' Bambi paid no attention to him. Overhead the yellow-bird sang from tree to tree, 'Good morning, I'm ha-appy.' Bambi did not answer. The thicket was very bright and shot through with sunbeams. Bambi did not stop to think about such things.

Suddenly there was a loud whir of wings. A

whole rainbow of gorgeous colours flashed from under Bambi's very feet and shone so close to his eyes that he stopped, dazzled. It was Jonello, the pheasant. He had flown up in terror, for Bambi had nearly stepped on him. He fled away, scolding.

'I never heard of such a thing,' he cried in his split, cackling voice. Bambi stood still in astonishment and stared after him.

'It turned out all right this time, but it really was inconsiderate,' said a soft twittering voice close to the ground. It was Jonellina, the pheasant's wife. She was sitting on the ground, hovering over her eggs. 'My husband was terribly frightened,' she went on in an irritable tone. 'And so was I. But I don't dare stir from this spot. I wouldn't stir from this spot no matter what happened. You could step on me and I wouldn't move.'

Bambi was a little embarrassed. 'I beg your pardon,' he stammered, 'I didn't mean to do it.'

'Oh, not at all,' the pheasant's wife replied. 'It was nothing so dreadful after all. But my husband and I are so nervous at present. You can understand why. . . .'

Bambi didn't understand why at all and went on. He was quieter now. The forest sang around him. The light grew more radiant and warmer.

The leaves on the bushes, the grass underfoot and the moist steaming earth began to smell more sweetly. Bambi's young strength swelled within him and streamed through all his limbs so that he walked around stiffly with awkward restrained movements like a mechanical thing.

He went up to a low alder shrub, and lifting his feet high, beat on the earth with such savage blows that the dust flew. His two sharp-pointed hoofs cut the turf that grew there. They scraped away the wood-vetch and leeks, the violets and snow bells, till the bare earth was furrowed in front of him. Every blow sounded dully.

Two moles, who were grubbing among the tangled roots of an old sycamore tree, grew anxious and, looking out, saw Bambi.

'That's a ridiculous way to do things,' said one mole. 'Who ever heard of anybody digging that way?'

The other mole drew down one corner of his mouth in a scornful sneer. 'He doesn't know anything, you can see that right off,' he said. 'But that's the way it is when people meddle with things they know nothing about.'

Suddenly Bambi listened, tossed up his head, listened again, and peered through the leaves. A flash of red showed through the branches. The prongs of an antler gleamed indistinctly. Bambi snorted. Whoever it might be who was circling around him, whether it was Karus or somebody else, didn't matter. 'Forward!' thought Bambi as he charged. 'I'll show them that I'm not afraid of them,' he thought as though suddenly exultant. 'I'll show them that they'd better look out for me.'

The branches rustled with the fury of his charge, the bushes cracked and broke. Then Bambi saw the other deer right in front of him. He did not recognize him, for everything was swimming before his eyes. He thought of nothing but, 'Forward!' His antlers lowered, he rushed on. All his strength was concentrated in his shoulders. He was ready for the blow. Then he smelt his opponent's hide. But he saw nothing ahead of him but the red wall of his flank. Then the other stag made a very slight turn and Bambi, not meeting the resistance he expected, charged past him into the empty air. He nearly went head over heels. He staggered, pulled himself together and made ready for a fresh onslaught.

Then he recognized the old stag.

Bambi was so astonished that he lost his self-possession. He was ashamed to run away as he would have liked to do. But he was also ashamed to stay there. He didn't move.

'Well?' asked the old stag, quietly and gently. His voice was so frank and yet so commanding it pierced Bambi to the heart. He was silent.

'Well?' the old stag repeated.

'I thought . . .' Bambi stammered, 'I thought . . . it was Ronno . . . or . . .' He stopped and risked a shy glance at the old stag. And this glance confused him still more. The old stag stood motionless and powerful. His head had turned completely white by now, and his proud dark eyes glowed in their depths.

'Why don't you charge me . . . ?' the old stag asked.

Bambi looked at him, filled with a wonderful ecstasy, and shaken by a mysterious tremor. He wanted to cry out, 'It's because I love you,' but he merely answered, 'I don't know. . . .'

The old stag looked at him. 'It's a long time since I've seen you,' he said. 'You've grown big and strong.'

Bambi did not answer. He trembled with joy. The old stag went on, examining him critically. Then he came unexpectedly up to Bambi, who was terribly frightened.

'Act bravely,' said the old stag.

He turned around and in the next moment had disappeared. Bambi remained in that place for a long while.

IT was summer and sizzling hot. The same longing he had felt before began to stir again in Bambi. But much more strongly now than then. It seethed in his blood and made him restless. He strayed far afield.

One day he met Faline. He met her quite unexpectedly, for his thoughts were so confused, his senses so clouded by the restless desire that raged within him, that he did not even recognize Faline. She was standing in front of him. Bambi stared at her speechless for a while. Then he said as though fascinated, 'How beautiful you have grown, Faline!'

'So you recognize me again?' Faline replied.

'How could I help recognizing you?' cried Bambi. 'Didn't we grow up together?'

Faline sighed. 'It's a long time since we've seen each other,' she said. Then she added, 'People grow to be strangers,' but she was already using her gay bantering tone again. They remained together.

'I used to walk on this path with my mother when I was a child,' Bambi said after a while.

'It leads to the meadow,' said Faline.

'I saw you for the first time on the meadow,' said Bambi a little solemnly. 'Do you remember?'

'Yes,' Faline replied. 'Gobo and me.' She sighed softly and said, 'Poor Gobo. . . .'

Bambi repeated, 'Poor Gobo.'

Then they began to talk about old times and asked each other every minute, 'Do you remember?' Each saw that the other still remembered everything. And they were both pleased at that.

'Do you remember how we used to play touch on the meadow?' Bambi reminisced.

'Yes, it was like this,' said Faline, and she was off like an arrow. At first Bambi hung back somewhat surprised, and then he rushed after her. 'Wait! wait!' he cried joyously.

'I can't wait,' teased Faline, 'I'm in too much of a hurry.' And bounding lightly away, she ran in a circle through the grass and bushes. At last Bambi caught up with her and barred the way. Then they stood quietly side by side. They laughed contentedly. Suddenly Faline leaped into the air as though someone had hit her, and bounded off anew. Bambi rushed after her. Faline raced around and around, always managing to elude him.

'Stop!' Bambi panted. 'I want to ask you something.'

Faline stopped.

'What do you want to ask me?' she inquired curiously.

Bambi was silent.

'O, so you're only fooling me,' said Faline, and started to turn away.

'No,' said Bambi quickly. 'Stop! stop! I wanted ... I wanted to ask you ... do you love me, Faline? ...'

She looked at him more curiously than before, and a little guardedly. 'I don't know,' she said.

'But you must know,' Bambi insisted. 'I know very well that I love you. I love you terribly, Faline. Tell me, don't you love me?'

'Perhaps I do,' she answered coyly.

'And will you stay with me?' Bambi demanded passionately.

'If you ask me nicely,' Faline said happily.

'Please do, Faline dear, beautiful, beloved Faline,' cried Bambi beside himself with love. 'Do you hear me? I want you with all my heart.'

'Then I'll certainly stay with you,' said Faline gently, and ran away.

In ecstasy, Bambi darted after her again. Faline fled straight across the meadow, swerved about and vanished into the thicket. But as

Bambi swerved to follow her there was a fierce rustling in the bushes and Karus sprang out.

'Halt!' he cried.

Bambi did not hear him. He was too busy with Faline. 'Let me pass,' he said hurriedly, 'I haven't time for you.'

'Get out,' Karus commanded angrily. 'Get away from here this minute or I'll shake you until there's no breath left in your body. I forbid you to follow Faline.'

The memory of last summer when he had been so often and so miserably hunted awakened in Bambi. Suddenly he became enraged. He did not say a word, but without waiting any longer rushed at Karus with his antlers lowered.

His charge was irresistible and, before he knew what had happened, Karus was lying in the grass. He was up again quicker than a flash, but was no sooner on his feet than a new attack made him stagger.

'Bambi,' he cried. 'Bam ...' he tried to cry

again, but a third blow, that glanced off his shoulder, nearly choked him with pain.

Karus sprang to one side in order to elude Bambi, who came rushing on again. Suddenly he felt strangely weak. At the same time he realized with a qualm that this was a life and death struggle. Cold terror seized him. He turned to flee from the silent Bambi, who came rushing after him. Karus knew that Bambi was furious and would kill him without mercy, and that thought numbed his wits completely. He fled from the path and, with a final effort, burst through the bushes. His one hope was of escape.

All at once Bambi ceased chasing him. Karus did not even notice this in his terror, and kept straight on through the bushes as fast as he could go. Bambi had stopped because he had heard Faline's shrill call. He listened as she called again in distress and fear. Suddenly he faced about and rushed back.

When he reached the meadow he saw Ronno pursuing Faline, who had fled into the thicket.

'Ronno,' cried Bambi. He did not even realize that he had called.

Ronno, who could not run very fast because of his lameness, stood still.

'O, there's our little Bambi,' he said scornfully, 'do you want something from me?'

'I do,' said Bambi quietly, but in a voice

which control and overpowering anger had completely altered. 'I want you to let Faline alone and to leave here immediately.'

'Is that all?' sneered Ronno. 'What an insolent gamin you've got to be. I wouldn't have thought it possible.'

'Ronno,' said Bambi still more softly, 'it's for your own sake. If you don't go now you'll be glad to run later, but then you'll never be able to run again.'

'Is that so?' cried Ronno in a rage. 'Do you dare to talk to me like that? It's because I limp, I suppose. Most people don't even notice it. Or maybe you think I'm afraid of you, too, because Karus was such a pitiful coward. I give you fair warning. . . .'

'No, Ronno,' Bambi broke in, 'I'll do all the warning. Go!' His voice trembled. 'I always liked you, Ronno. I always thought you were very clever and respected you because you were older than I am. I tell you once and for all, go. I haven't any patience left.'

'It's a pity you have so little patience,' Ronno said with a sneer, 'a great pity for you, my boy. But be easy, I'll soon finish you off. You won't have long to wait. Maybe you've forgotten how often I used to chase you.'

At the thought of that Bambi had nothing more to say. Nothing could hold him back. Like a wild beast he tore at Ronno, who met him with his head lowered. They charged together with a crash. Ronno stood firm but wondered why Bambi did not blench back. The sudden charge had dazed him, for he had not expected that Bambi would attack him first. Uneasily he felt Bambi's giant strength and saw that he must keep himself well in hand.

He tried to turn a trick as they stood forehead pressed against forehead. He suddenly shifted his weight so that Bambi lost his balance and staggered forward.

Bambi braced with his hind legs and hurled himself on Ronno with redoubled fury before he had time to regain his footing. A prong broke from Ronno's antlers with a loud snap. Ronno thought his forehead was shattered. The sparks danced before his eyes and there was a roaring in his ears. The next moment a terrific blow tore open his shoulder. His breath failed him and he fell to the ground with Bambi standing over him furiously.

'Let me go,' Ronno groaned.

Bambi charged blindly at him. His eyes flashed. He seemed to have no thought of mercy.

'Please stop,' whined Ronno pitifully. 'Don't you know that I'm lame? I was only joking. Spare me. Can't you take a joke?'

Bambi let him alone without a word. Ronno rose warily. He was bleeding and his legs tottered. He slunk off in silence.

Bambi started for the thicket to look for Faline, but she came out of her own accord. She had been standing at the edge of the woods and had seen it all.

'That was wonderful,' she said, laughing. Then she added softly and seriously, 'I love you.'

They walked on very happily together.

ONE day they went to look for the little clearing in the depth of the woods where Bambi had last met the old stag. Bambi told Faline all about the old stag and grew enthusiastic.

'Maybe we'll meet him again,' he said. 'I'd like you to see him.'

'It would be nice,' said Faline boldly. 'I'd really like to chat with him once myself.' But she wasn't telling the truth for, though she was very inquisitive, she was afraid of the old stag.

The twilight was already dusky grey. Sunset was near.

They walked softly side by side where the leaves hung quivering on the shrubs and bushes and permitted a clear view in all directions. Presently there was a rustling sound near by. They stopped and looked towards it. Then the old stag marched slowly and powerfully through the bushes into the clearing. In the drab twilight he seemed like a gigantic grey shadow.

Faline uttered an involuntary cry. Bambi controlled himself. He was terrified, too, and a cry stuck in his throat. But Faline's voice sounded so helpless that pity seized him and made him want to comfort her.

'What's the matter?' he whispered solicitously, while his voice quavered; 'what's the matter with you? He isn't going to hurt us.'

Faline simply shrieked again.

'Don't be so terribly upset, beloved,' Bambi pleaded. 'It's ridiculous to be so frightened by him. After all he's one of our own family.'

But Faline wouldn't be comforted. She stood stock-still, staring at the stag, who went along unconcerned. Then she shrieked and shrieked.

'Pull yourself together,' Bambi begged. 'What will he think of us?'

But Faline was not to be quieted. 'He can think what he likes,' she cried, bleating again. 'Ah-oh! Baoah! . . . It's terrible to be so big!'

She bleated again, 'Baoh! Leave me,' she went on, 'I can't help it, I have to bleat. Baoh! baoh! baoh!'

The stag was standing in the little clearing, looking for tidbits in the grass.

Fresh courage came to Bambi, who had one eye on the hysterical Faline, the other on the placid stag. With the encouragement he had given Faline he had conquered his own fears.

He began to reproach himself for the pitiful state he was in whenever he saw the old stag, a state of mingled terror and excitement, admiration and submissiveness.

'It's perfectly absurd,' he said with painful decision. 'I'm going straight over to tell him who I am.'

'Don't,' cried Faline. 'Don't! Ba-oh! Something terrible will happen. Baoh!'

'I'm going, anyway,' answered Bambi.

The stag who was feasting so calmly, not paying the slightest attention to the weeping Faline, seemed altogether too haughty to him. He felt offended and humiliated. 'I'm going,' he said. 'Be quiet. You'll see, nothing will happen. Wait for me here.'

He went, but Faline did not wait. She hadn't

the least desire or courage to do so. She faced about and ran away crying, for she thought it was the best thing she could do. Bambi could hear her going farther and farther away, bleating, 'Ba-oh! Baoh!'

Bambi would gladly have followed her. But that was no longer possible. He pulled himself together and went forward.

Through the branches he saw the stag standing in the clearing, his head close to the ground. Bambi felt his heart pounding as he stepped out.

The stag immediately lifted his head and looked at him. Then he gazed absently straight ahead again. The way in which the stag gazed into space, as though no one else were there, seemed as haughty to Bambi as the way he had stared at him.

Bambi did not know what to do. He had come with the firm intention of speaking to the stag. He wanted to say, 'Good day, I am Bambi. May I ask to know your honourable name also?'

Yes, it had all seemed very easy, but now it appeared that the affair was not so simple. What good were the best of intentions now? Bambi did not want to seem ill-bred as he would be if he went off without saying a word. But he did not want to seem forward either, and he would be if he began the conversation.

The stag was wonderfully majestical. It delighted Bambi and made him feel humble. He tried in vain to arouse his courage and kept asking himself, 'Why do I let him frighten me? Am I not just as good as he is?' But it was no use. Bambi continued to be frightened and felt in his heart of hearts that he really was not as good as the old stag. Far from it. He felt wretched and had to use all his strength to keep himself steady.

The old stag looked at him and thought, 'He's handsome, he's really charming, so delicate, so poised, so elegant in his whole bearing. I must not stare at him, though. It really isn't the thing to do. Besides, it might embarrass him.' So he stared over Bambi's head into the empty air again.

'What a haughty look,' thought Bambi. 'It's unbearable, the opinion such people have of themselves.'

The stag was thinking, 'I'd like to talk to him, he looks so sympathetic. How stupid never to speak to people we don't know.' He looked thoughtfully ahead of him.

'I might as well be air,' said Bambi to himself. 'This fellow acts as though he were the only thing on the face of the earth.'

'What should I say to him?' the old stag was wondering. 'I'm not used to talking. I'd say some-

thing stupid and make myself ridiculous ...
for he's undoubtedly very clever.'

Bambi pulled himself together and looked
fixedly at the stag. 'How splendid he is,' he
thought despairingly.

'Well, some other time, perhaps,' the stag
decided, and walked off dissatisfied but majes-
tic.

Bambi remained filled with bitterness.

THE forest sweltered under a scorching sun. Since it rose it had driven even the tiniest cloudlet from the sky, and shone all alone in the wide blue depths that were pallid now with heat. Over the meadows and the tree-tops the air quivered in glassy, transparent ripples as it does over a flame. Not a leaf was moving, not a blade of grass. The birds were silent, and sat hidden among the shady leaves, never stirring from their places. All the paths and trails in the thicket were empty. Not a creature was abroad. The forest lay as though hurt by the blinding light. The earth and the trees, the bushes, the beasts, breathed in the intense heat with a kind of sluggish satisfaction.

Bambi was asleep.

He had made merry with Faline all night. He had pranced around with her until broad daylight, and in his bliss had even forgotten to eat. But he had grown so tired that he did not feel hungry any more. His eyes fell shut. He lay down where he happened to be standing, in the middle of the bushes, and fell asleep at once.

The bitter acrid odour that streamed from the sun-warmed juniper, and the penetrating scent of spurge laurel, mounted to his head while he slept and gave him new strength. Suddenly he awoke in a daze. Had Faline called him? Bambi looked around. He remembered seeing Faline as he lay down, standing close beside him near the white-thorn, nibbling the leaves. He had supposed she would remain near him, but she was gone. Apparently she had grown tired of being alone by now and was calling for him to come and look for her.

As Bambi listened he wondered how long he could have slept and how often Faline had called. He wasn't sure. Veils of sleep still clouded his thought.

Then she called again. With a side-wise spring Bambi turned in the direction the sound came from. Then he heard it again. And suddenly he felt perfectly happy. He was wonderfully refreshed, quieted and strengthened, but racked by a terrific appetite.

The call came again clearly, thin as a bird's twittering, tender and full of longing. 'Come, come!', it said.

'Yes, that was her voice. That was Faline. Bambi rushed away so fast that the dry branches barely crackled as he burst through the bushes and the hot green leaves scarcely rustled.

But he had to stop short in the midst of his course, and swerve to one side, for the old stag was standing there, barring his path.

Bambi had no time for anything but love. The old stag was indifferent to him now. He would meet him again somewhere later on. He had no time for old stags now, however noble they might be. He had thoughts for Faline alone. He greeted the stag hastily and tried to hurry by.

'Where are you going?' asked the old stag earnestly.

Bambi was somewhat embarrassed and tried to think of an evasion, but he changed his mind and answered truthfully, 'to her.'

'Don't go,' said the old stag.

For a second a single angry spark flared up in Bambi's mind. Not go to Faline? How could the mean old stag ask that? 'I'll simply run off,' Bambi thought. And he looked quickly at the old stag. But the deep look that met him in the old stag's eyes held him fast. He quivered with impatience but he did not run away.

'She's calling me,' he said in explanation. He said it in a tone which clearly bleated, 'Don't keep me talking here.'

'No,' said the old stag, 'she isn't calling.'

The call came once again, thin as a bird's twittering, 'Come!'

'Listen,' Bambi cried excitedly, 'there it is again.'

'I hear it,' said the old stag, nodding.

'Well, good-bye,' Bambi flung back hurriedly.

'Stop,' the old stag commanded.

'What do you want?' cried Bambi, beside himself with impatience. 'Let me go. I have no time. Please, Faline is calling. . . . You ought to see that. . . .'

'I tell you,' the old stag said, 'that it isn't she.'

Bambi was desperate. 'But,' he said, 'I know her voice.'

'Listen to me,' the old stag went on.

Again the call came. Bambi felt the ground burning under his feet. 'Later,' he pleaded, 'I'll come back.'

'No,' said the old stag sadly, 'you'll never come back, never again.'

The call came again. 'I must go! I must go!' cried Bambi, who was nearly out of his wits.

'Then,' the old stag declared in a commanding voice, 'we'll go together.'

'Quickly,' cried Bambi, and bounded off.

'No, slowly,' commanded the old stag in a voice that forced Bambi to obey. 'Stay behind me. Move one step at a time.'

The old stag began to move forward. Bambi

followed, sighing with impatience.

'Listen,' said the old stag without stopping, 'no matter how often that call comes, don't stir from my side. If it's Faline you'll get to hear her soon enough. But it isn't Faline. Don't let yourself be tempted. Everything depends now on whether you trust me or not.'

Bambi did not dare to resist, and surrendered in silence.

The old stag advanced slowly and Bambi followed him. O how cleverly the old stag moved! Not a sound came from under his hoofs. Not a leaf was disturbed. Not a twig snapped. And yet they were gliding through thick bushes, slinking through the ancient tangled thicket. Bambi was amazed and had to admire him in spite of his impatience. He had never dreamed that anybody could move like that.

The call came again and again. The old stag stood still, listening and nodding his head. Bambi stood beside him, shaken with desire, and suffering from restraint. He could not understand it at all.

Several times the old stag stopped, although no call had come, and lifted his head, listening and nodding, Bambi heard nothing. The old stag turned away from the direction of the call and made a detour. Bambi raged inwardly because of it.

The call came again and again. At last they drew nearer to it, then still nearer. At last they were quite near.

The old stag whispered, 'No matter what you see, don't move, do you hear? Watch everything I do and act just as I do, cautiously. And don't lose your head.'

They went a few steps farther and suddenly that sharp arresting scent that Bambi knew so well struck them full in the face. He swallowed so much of it that he nearly cried out. He stood as though rooted to the ground. For a moment his heart seemed pounding in his throat. The old stag stood calmly beside him and motioned with his eyes.

He was standing there.

He was standing quite close to them leaning against the trunk of an oak, hidden by hazel bushes. He was calling softly, 'Come, come!'

Bambi was completely bewildered. He was so terrified that he began to understand only by degrees that it was He who was imitating Faline's voice. It was He who was calling, 'Come, come!'

Cold terror shot through Bambi's body. The idea of flight gripped him and tugged at his heart.

'Be still,' whispered the old stag quickly and commandingly as if he meant to forestall any outbreak of fear. Bambi controlled himself with an effort.

The old stag looked at him a little scornfully at first, it seemed to Bambi. He noticed it in spite of the state he was in. But the stag changed at once to a serious and kindly look.

Bambi peered out with blinking eyes to where He was standing, and felt as if he could not bear His horrible presence much longer.

As if he had read this thought, the old stag whispered to him, 'Let's go back,' and turned about.

They glided away cautiously. The old stag moved with a marvellous zigzag course whose purpose Bambi did not understand. Again he followed with painfully controlled impatience. The longing for Faline had harassed him on the way over; now the impulse to flee was beating through his veins.

But the old stag walked on slowly, stopping and listening. He would begin a new zigzag, then stop again, going very slowly ahead.

By this time they were far from the danger spot. 'If he stops again,' thought Bambi, 'it ought to be all right to speak to him by now, and I'll thank him.'

But at that moment the old stag vanished under his very eyes into a thick tangle of undergrowth. Not a leaf stirred, not a twig snapped as the stag slipped away.

Bambi followed and tried to get through as noiselessly, and to avoid every sound with as much skill. But he was not so lucky. The leaves swished gently, the boughs bent against his flanks and sprang up again with a loud twang; dry branches broke against his chest with sharp piercing snaps.

'He saved my life,' Bambi kept thinking. 'What can I say to him?'

But the old stag was nowhere to be seen. Bambi came out of the bushes. Around him was a sea of yellow flowering golden-rod. He raised his head and looked around. Not a leaf was moving as far as he could see. He was all alone.

Freed from all control, the impulse to flee suddenly carried him away. The golden-rods parted with a loud swish beneath his bounding hoofs as though under the stroke of a scythe.

After wandering about for a long time he found Faline. He was breathless, tired and happy and deeply stirred.

'Please, beloved,' he said, 'please don't ever call me again. We'll search until we find each other, but please don't ever call me ... for I can't resist your voice.'

A few days later they were walking carefree together through an oak thicket on the far side of the meadow. They had to cross the meadow in order to reach their old trail where the tall oak stood.

As the bushes grew thinner around them they stopped and peered out. Something red was moving near the oak. Both of them looked at it.

'Who can it be?' whispered Bambi.

'Probably Ronno or Karus,' said Faline.

Bambi doubted it. 'They don't dare come near me any more,' Bambi said, peering sharply ahead. 'No,' he decided, 'that's not Karus or Ronno. It's a stranger.'

Faline agreed, surprised, and very curious. 'Yes,' she said, 'it's a stranger. I see it, too, now. How curious!'

They watched him.

'How carelessly he acts,' exclaimed Faline.

'Stupid,' said Bambi, 'really stupid. He acts like a little child, as if there were no danger.'

'Let's go over,' Faline proposed. Her curiosity was getting the better of her.

'All right,' Bambi answered. 'Let's go, I want to have a better look at the fellow.'

They took a few steps and then Faline stopped. 'Suppose he wants to fight you,' she said. 'He's strong.'

'Bah,' said Bambi, holding his head cocked and putting on a disdainful air, 'look at the little antlers he has. Should I be afraid of that? The fellow is fat and sleek enough, but is he strong? I don't think so. Come along.'

They went on.

The stranger was busy nibbling meadow grass and did not notice them until they were a good way across the meadow. Then he ran forward to meet them. He gave joyful playful skips that made a curiously childish impression. Bambi and Faline stopped, surprised, and waited for him. When he was a few steps off he stood still likewise.

After a while he asked, 'Don't you know me?'

Bambi had lowered his head prepared for battle. 'Do you know us?' he retorted.

The stranger interrupted him. 'Bambi,' he cried reproachfully, yet confidently.

Bambi was startled to hear his name spoken. The sound of that voice stirred an old memory in his heart. But Faline had rushed towards the stranger.

'Gobo,' she cried, and became speechless. She stood there silent without moving. She couldn't breathe.

'Faline,' said Gobo softly, 'Faline, sister, you knew me anyway.' He went to her and kissed her mouth. The tears were running down his cheeks. Faline was crying too, and couldn't speak.

'Well, Gobo,' Bambi began. His voice trembled and he felt very bewildered. He was deeply moved and very much surprised. 'Well, so you're not dead,' he said.

Gobo burst out laughing. 'You see that I'm not dead,' he said, 'at least I think you can see that I'm not.'

'But what happened that time in the snow?' Bambi persisted.

'O then?' Gobo said thoughtfully. 'He rescued me then.'

'And where have you been all this time?' asked Faline in astonishment.

'With Him,' Gobo replied, 'I've been with Him all the time.'

He grew silent and looked at Faline and at Bambi. Their helpless astonishment delighted him. Then he added, 'Yes, my dears, I've seen a lot more than all of you put together in your old forest.' He sounded somewhat boastful, but they paid no attention to it. They were still too much absorbed in their great surprise.

'Tell us about it,' cried Faline, beside herself with joy.

'O,' said Gobo with satisfaction, 'I could talk all day about it and never reach the end.'

'Well then, go ahead and talk,' Bambi urged.

Gobo turned to Faline and grew serious. 'Is mother still alive?' he asked timidly and softly.

'Yes,' cried Faline gladly. 'She's alive, but I haven't seen her for a long while.'

'I'm going to see her right away,' said Gobo with decision. 'Are you coming too?'

They all went.

They did not speak another word the whole way. Bambi and Faline felt Gobo's impatient longing to see his mother, so both of them kept silent. Gobo walked ahead hurriedly and did not speak. They let him do as he liked.

Only sometimes when he hurried blindly over a cross-trail or when, in a sudden burst of speed, he took the wrong turning, they called gently to him. 'This way,' Bambi would whisper, or Faline would say, 'No, no, we go this way now.'

A number of times they had to cross wide clearings. They noticed that Gobo never stopped at the edge of the thicket, never peered around for a moment when he walked into the open, but simply ran out without any precaution. Bambi and Faline exchanged astonished glances whenever this happened, but they never said a word and followed Gobo with some hesitation. They had to wander around some time and search high and low.

Gobo recollected his childhood paths at once. He was delighted with himself, never realizing that Bambi and Faline were leading him. He looked around at them and called, 'How do you like the way I can still find my way?' They did not say anything, but they exchanged glances again.

Soon afterwards they came to a small leafy hollow. 'Look,' cried Faline, and glided in. Gobo followed her and stopped. It was the glade in which they were both born and had lived with their mother as little children. Gobo and Faline looked into each other's eyes. They did not say a word. But Faline kissed her brother gently on the mouth. Then they hurried on.

They walked to and fro for a good hour. The sun shone brighter and brighter through the branches and the forest grew stiller and stiller. It was the time for lying down and resting. But Gobo didn't feel tired. He walked swiftly ahead, breathing deeply with impatience and excitement, and gazed aimlessly about him. He shrank together whenever a weasel slunk through the bushes at his feet. He nearly stepped on the pheasants, and when they scolded him, flying up with a loud flapping of wings, he was terribly frightened. Bambi marvelled at the strange, blind way Gobo moved around.

Presently Gobo stopped and turned to them both. 'She isn't anywhere here,' he cried in despair.

Faline soothed him. 'We'll soon find her,' she said, deeply moved, 'soon, Gobo.' She looked at him. He still had that dejected look she knew so well.

'Shall we call her?' she asked, smiling. 'Shall we call her the way we used to when we were children?'

Bambi went away a few steps. Then he saw Aunt Ena. She had already settled herself to rest and was lying quietly in a nearby hazel-bush.

'At last,' he said to himself. At the same moment Gobo and Faline came up. All three of them stood together and looked at Ena. She had raised her head quietly and looked sleepily back at them.

Gobo took a few hesitating steps and cried softly, 'Mother.'

She was on her feet in a flash and stood as though transfixed. Gobo sprang to her quickly. 'Mother,' he began again. He tried to speak but couldn't utter a word.

His mother looked deep into his eyes. Her rigid

body began to move. Wave after wave of trembling broke over her shoulders and down her back.

She did not ask any questions. She did not want any explanation or history. She kissed Gobo slowly on the mouth. She kissed his cheeks and his neck. She bathed him tirelessly in her kisses, as she had when he was born.

Bambi and Faline had gone away.

They were all standing around in the middle of the thicket in a little clearing. Gobo was talking to them.

Even Friend Hare was there. Full of astonishment, he would lift one spoonlike ear, listen attentively, and let it fall back, only to lift it again at once.

The magpie was perched on the lowest branch of a young beech and listened in amazement. The jay was sitting restlessly on an ash opposite and screamed every once in a while in wonder.

A few friendly pheasants had brought their wives and children and were stretching their necks in surprise as they listened. At times they would jerk them in again, turning their heads this way and that in speechless wonder.

The squirrel had scurried up and was gesticulating, wild with excitement. At times he would slide to the ground, at times he would run up some tree or other. Or he would balance with his tail erect and display his white chest. Every now and again he tried to interrupt Gobo and say something, but he was always told sternly to keep quiet.

Gobo told how he had lain helpless in the snow waiting to die.

'The dogs found me,' he said. 'Dogs are terrible. They are certainly the most terrible creatures in the world. Their jaws drip blood and their bark is pitiless and full of anger.' He looked all around the circle and continued, 'Well, since then I've played with them just as I would with one of you.' He was very proud. 'I don't need to be afraid of them any more, I'm good friends with them now. Nevertheless when they begin to grow angry, I have a roaring in my ears and my heart stops beating. But they don't really mean any harm by it and, as I said, I'm a good friend of theirs. But their bark is terribly loud.'

'Go on,' Faline urged.

Gobo looked at her. 'Well,' he said, 'they would have torn me to pieces, but He came.'

Gobo paused. The others hardly breathed.

'Yes,' said Gobo, 'He came. He called off the dogs and they quieted down at once. He called them again and they crouched motionless at His feet. Then He picked me up. I screamed, but He petted me. He held me in His arms. He didn't hurt me. And then He carried me away.'

Faline interrupted him. 'What does "carry" mean?' she asked.

Gobo began to explain it in great detail.

'It's very simple,' Bambi broke in, 'look at what the squirrel does when he takes a nut and carries it off.'

The squirrel tried to speak again. 'A cousin of mine . . .' he began eagerly. But the others cried out at once, 'Be still, be still, let Gobo go on.'

The squirrel had to keep quiet. He was desperate and, pressing his forepaws against his white chest, he tried to begin a conversation with the magpie. 'As I was saying, a cousin of mine . . .' he began. But the magpie simply turned her back on him.

Gobo told of wonders. 'Outside it will be cold and the storm is howling. But inside there's not a breath of wind and it's as warm as in summertime,' he said.

'Akh!' screamed the jay.

'The rain may be pouring outside so that everything is flooded. But not a drop of it gets inside and you keep dry.'

The pheasants craned their necks and twisted their heads.

'Everything outside may be snowed under, but inside I was warm,' said Gobo, 'I was even hot. They gave me hay to eat and chestnuts, potatoes and turnips, whatever I wanted.'

'Hay?' they all cried at once, amazed, incredulous and excited.

'Sweet, new-mown hay,' Gobo repeated calmly, and gazed triumphantly around.

The squirrel's voice cut in, 'A cousin of mine . . .'

'Keep quiet,' cried the others.

'Where does He get hay and all the rest of the things in winter?' asked Faline eagerly.

'He grows them,' Gobo answered. 'He grows what He wants and keeps what He wants.'

Faline went on questioning him. 'Weren't you ever afraid, Gobo, when you were with Him?' she asked.

Gobo smiled a very superior smile. 'No, dear Faline,' he said, 'not any more. I got to know that He wouldn't hurt me. Why should I have been afraid? You all think He's wicked. But He isn't wicked. If He loves anybody or if anybody serves Him, He's good to him. Wonderfully good. Nobody in the world can be as kind as He can.'

While Gobo was talking that way the old stag suddenly stepped noiselessly from the bushes.

Gobo didn't notice him and went on talking. But the others saw the old stag and held their breath in awe.

The old stag stood motionless, watching Gobo with deep and serious eyes.

Gobo said, 'Not only He, but all His children loved me. His wife and all of them used to pet me and play with me.' He broke off suddenly. He had seen the old stag.

A silence followed.

Then the old stag asked in his quiet commanding voice, 'What kind of a band is that you have on your neck?'

Everybody looked at it and noticed for the first time the dark strip of braided horse-hair around Gobo's neck.

Gobo answered uneasily, 'That? Why that's part of the halter I wore. It's His halter and it's the greatest honour to wear His halter, it's . . .' He grew confused and stammered.

Everyone was silent. The old stag looked at Gobo for a long time, piercingly and sadly.

'You poor thing!' he said softly at last, and turned and was gone.

In the astonished silence that followed, the squirrel began to chatter again. 'As I was saying, a cousin of mine stayed with Him, too. He caught him and shut him up, oh, for the longest while, till one day my father . . .'

But nobody was listening to the squirrel. They were all walking away.

ONE day Marena appeared again.

She was almost full-grown the winter that Gobo disappeared, but she had hardly ever been seen since, for she lived alone, going her own ways.

She had stayed slender and looked quite young. But she was quiet and serious and gentler than any of the others. She had heard from the squirrel and the jay, the magpie and the thrushes and pheasants that Gobo had returned from his wonderful adventures. So she came back to see him.

Gobo's mother was very proud and happy over her visit. Gobo's mother had grown rather proud of her good fortune. She was delighted to hear the whole forest talking about her son. She basked in his glory and wanted everybody to know that her Gobo was the cleverest, ablest and best deer living.

'What do you think of him, Marena?' she ex-

claimed. 'What do you think of our Gobo?' She
didn't wait for an answer but went on, 'Do you
remember how old Nettla said he wasn't worth
much because he shivered a little in the cold? Do
you remember how she prophesied that he'd be
nothing but a care to me?'

'Well,' Marena answered, 'you've had plenty
of worry over Gobo.'

'That's all over with now,' his mother exclaimed. She wondered how people could still
remember such things. 'O, I'm sorry for poor old
Nettla. What a pity that she couldn't live to see
what my Gobo's become!'

'Yes, poor old Nettla,' said Marena softly, 'it's
too bad about her.'

Gobo liked to hear his mother praise him like
that. It pleased him. He stood around and basked
as happily in her praises as in the sunshine.

'Even the old Prince came to see Gobo,' his
mother told Marena. She whispered it as though
it were something solemn and mysterious. 'He
never let anyone so much as get a glimpse of him
before, but he came on account of Gobo.'

'Why did he call me a poor thing?' Gobo broke
in in a discontented tone. 'I'd like to know what
he meant by that.'

'Don't think about it,' his mother said to comfort him, 'he's old and queer.'

But at last Gobo meant to ease his mind. 'All

day long it keeps running through my head,' he said. 'Poor thing! I'm not a poor thing. I'm very lucky. I've seen more and been through more than all the rest of you put together. I've seen more of the world and I know more about life than anyone in the forest. What do you think, Marena?'

'Yes,' she said, 'no one can deny that.'

From then on Marena and Gobo were always together.

BAMBI went to look for the old stag. He roamed around all night long. He wandered till the sun rose and dawn found him on unbeaten trails without Faline.

He was still drawn to Faline at times. At times he loved her just as much as ever. Then he liked to roam about with her, to listen to her chatter, to browse with her on the meadow or at the edge of the thicket. But she no longer satisfied him completely.

Before, when he was with Faline, he hardly ever remembered his meetings with the old stag, and when he did it was only casually. Now he was looking for him and felt an inexplicable desire driving him to find him. He only thought of Faline between whiles. He could always be with her if he wanted to. He did not much care to stay with the others. Gobo or Aunt Ena he avoided when he could.

The words the old stag had let fall about Gobo kept ringing in Bambi's ears. They made a peculiarly deep impression on him. Gobo had affected him strangely from the very first day of his return. Bambi didn't know why, but there was something painful to him in Gobo's bearing. Bambi was ashamed of Gobo without knowing why. And he was afraid for him, again without knowing why. Whenever he was together with his harmless, vain, self-conscious and self-satisfied Gobo, the words kept running through his head, 'Poor thing!' He couldn't get rid of them.

But one dark night when Bambi had again delighted the screech-owl by assuring him how badly he was frightened, it suddenly occurred to him to ask, 'Do you happen to know where the old stag is now?'

The screech-owl answered in his cooing voice that he didn't have the least idea in the world. But Bambi perceived that he simply didn't want to tell.

'No,' he said, 'I don't believe you, you're too clever. You know everything that's happening in the forest. You certainly must know where the old stag is hiding.'

The screech-owl, who was all fluffed up, smoothed his feathers against his body and made himself small. 'Of course I know,' he cooed still more softly, 'but I oughtn't to tell you, I really oughtn't.'

Bambi began to plead. 'I won't give you

away,' he said. 'How could I when I respect you so much?'

The owl became a lovely, soft grey-brown ball again and rolled his big cunning eyes a little as he always did when he felt in a good humour. 'So you really do respect me,' he asked, 'and why, pray?'

Bambi did not hesitate. 'Because you're so wise,' he said sincerely, 'and so good-natured and friendly, besides. And because you're so clever at frightening people. It's so very clever to frighten people, so very, very clever. I wish I could do it, it would be a great help to me.'

The screech-owl had sunk his bill into his downy breast and was happy.

'Well,' he said, 'I know that the old stag would be glad to see you.'

'Do you really think so?' cried Bambi, while his heart began to beat faster for joy.

'Yes, I'm sure of it,' the owl answered. 'He'd be glad to see you, and I think I can venture to tell you where he is now.'

He laid his feathers close to his body and suddenly grew thin again.

'Do you know the deep ditch where the willows stand?'

Bambi nodded, yes.

'Do you know the young oak thicket on the farther side?'

'No,' Bambi confessed, 'I've never been on the farther side?'

'Well, listen carefully then,' the owl whispered. 'There's an oak thicket on the far side. Go through that. Then there are bushes, hazel and silver poplar, thorn and hemlock. In the midst of them is an old uprooted beech. You'll have to hunt for it. It's not so easy to see it from your height as it is from the air. You'll find him under the trunk. But don't tell him I told you.'

'Under the trunk?' said Bambi.

'Yes,' the screech-owl laughed, 'there's a hollow in the ground there. The trunk lies right across it. And he sleeps under the trunk.'

'Thank you,' said Bambi sincerely. 'I don't know if I can find it, but I'm very grateful anyhow.' He ran quickly away.

The screech-owl flew noiselessly after him and began to hoot right beside him. 'Oy! Oy!' Bambi shrank together.

'Did I frighten you?' asked the owl.

'Yes,' he stammered, and that time he told the truth.

The owl cooed with satisfaction and said, 'I only wanted to remind you again. Don't tell him I told you.'

'Of course not,' Bambi assured him, and ran on.

When Bambi reached the ditch the old stag

rose before him out of the pitch black night, so noiselessly and suddenly that Bambi drew back in terror.

'I'm no longer where you were going to look for me,' said the stag.

Bambi was silent.

'What is it you want?' asked the stag.

'Nothing,' Bambi stammered, 'nothing, excuse me, nothing at all.'

After a while the old stag spoke and his voice sounded gentle. 'This isn't the first time you've been looking for me,' he said.

He waited. Bambi did not answer. The old stag went on, 'Yesterday you passed close by me twice, and again this morning, very close.'

'Why,' said Bambi, gathering courage, 'why did you say that about Gobo?'

'Do you think that I was wrong?'

'No,' cried Bambi sorrowfully, 'no, I feel that you were right.'

The old stag gave a barely perceptible nod and his eyes rested on Bambi more kindly than ever before.

'But why?' Bambi said. 'I don't understand it.'

'It's enough that you feel it. You will understand it later,' the old stag said. 'Good-bye.'

Everybody soon saw that Gobo had habits which seemed strange and suspicious to the rest of them. He slept at night when the others were awake. But in the daytime when the rest of them were looking for places to sleep in, he was wide awake and went walking. When he felt like it, he would even go out of the thicket without any hesitation and stand with perfect peace of mind in the bright sunshine on the meadow.

Bambi found it impossible to keep silent any longer. 'Don't you ever think of the danger?' he asked.

'No,' Gobo said simply, 'there isn't any for me.'

'You forget, my dear Bambi,' Gobo's mother broke in, 'you forget that He's a friend of Gobo's. Gobo can take chances that the rest of you cannot take.' She was very proud.

Bambi did not say anything more.

One day Gobo said to him, 'You know, it seems strange to me to eat when and where I like.'

Bambi did not understand. 'Why is it strange, we all do it,' he said.

'O, you do,' said Gobo superiorly, 'but I'm a little different. I'm accustomed to having my food brought to me or to being called when it's ready.'

Bambi stared pityingly at Gobo. He looked at Faline and Marena and Aunt Ena. But they were all smiling and admiring Gobo.

'I think it will be hard for you to get accustomed to the winter, Gobo,' Faline began, 'we don't have hay or turnips or potatoes in the winter-time.'

'That's true,' answered Gobo reflectively. 'I hadn't thought about that yet. I can't even imagine how it would feel. It must be dreadful.'

Bambi said quietly, 'It isn't dreadful. It's only hard.'

'Well,' Gobo declared grandly, 'if it gets too hard for me I'll simply go back to Him. Why should I go hungry? There's no need for that.'

Bambi turned away without a word and walked off.

When Gobo was alone again with Marena he began to talk about Bambi. 'He doesn't understand me,' he said. 'Poor old Bambi thinks I'm still the silly little Gobo that I once was. He can never get used to the fact that I've become something unusual. Danger! ... What does he mean by danger? He means well enough by me, but danger is something for him and the likes of him, not for me.'

Marena agreed with him. She loved him and Gobo loved her and they were both very happy.

'Well,' he said to her, 'nobody understands me the way you do. But anyhow I can't complain. I'm respected and honoured by everybody. But you understand me best of all. When I tell the others how good He is, they listen and they don't think I'm lying, but they stick to their opinion that He's dreadful.'

'I've always believed in him,' said Marena dreamily.

'Really?' Gobo replied airily.

'Do you remember the day when they left you lying in the snow?' Marena went on. 'I said that day that some time He'd come to the forest to play with us.'

'No,' Gobo replied, yawning, 'I don't remember that.'

A few weeks passed, and one morning Bambi and Faline, Gobo and Marena were standing together again in the old familiar hazel thicket. Bambi and Faline were just returning from their wanderings, intending to look for their hiding place, when they met Gobo and Marena. Gobo was about to go out on the meadow.

'Stay with us instead,' said Bambi, 'the sun will soon be rising and then nobody will go out in the open.'

'Nonsense,' said Gobo scornfully, 'if nobody else will go, I will.'

He went on, Marena following him.

Bambi and Faline had stopped. 'Come along,' said Bambi angrily to Faline, 'come along. Let him do what he pleases.'

They were going on, but suddenly the jay screamed loudly from the far side of the meadow. With a bound Bambi had turned and was running after Gobo. Right by the oak he caught up with him and Marena.

'Did you hear that?' he cried to him.

'What?' asked Gobo, puzzled.

Again the jay screamed on the far side of the meadow.

'Did you hear that?' Bambi repeated.

'No,' said Gobo calmly.

'That means danger,' Bambi persisted.

A magpie began to chatter loudly and, immediately after her, another and then a third. Then the jay screamed again and far overhead the crows gave warning.

Faline began to plead. 'Don't go out there, Gobo! It's dangerous.'

Even Marena begged, 'Stay here. Stay here today, beloved one. It's dangerous.'

Gobo stood there, smiling in his superior way. 'Dangerous! dangerous! What has that to do with me?' he asked.

His pressing need gave Bambi an idea. 'At least let Marena go first,' he said, 'so we can find out. . . .'

He hadn't finished before Marena had slipped out.

All three stood and looked at her, Bambi and Faline breathlessly, Gobo with obvious patience, as if to let the others enjoy their foolish whims.

They saw how Marena walked across the meadow step by step, with hesitant feet, her head up. She peered and snuffed in all directions. Suddenly she turned like a flash with one high bound and, as though a cyclone had struck her, rushed back into the thicket.

'It's He, He,' she whispered, her voice choking with terror. She was trembling in every limb. 'I – I saw Him,' she stammered, 'it's He. He's standing over by the elders.'

'Come,' cried Bambi, 'come quickly.'

'Come,' Faline pleaded. And Marena, who could hardly speak, whispered, 'Please come now, Gobo, please.'

But Gobo remained unmoved. 'Run as much as you like,' he said, 'I won't stop you. If He's there I want to talk with Him.'

Gobo could not be dissuaded.

They stood and watched how he went out. They stayed there, moved by his great confidence, while at the same time a terrible fear for him gripped them.

Gobo was standing boldly on the meadow looking around for the elders. Then he seemed to see them and to have discovered Him. Then the thunder crashed.

Gobo leaped into the air at the report. He suddenly turned around and fled back to the thicket, staggering as he came.

They still stood there, petrified with terror, while he came on. They heard him gasping for breath. And as he did not stop but bounded wildly forward, they turned and surrounded him and all took flight.

But poor Gobo dropped to the ground. Marena

stopped close to him, Bambi and Faline a little farther off, ready to flee.

Gobo lay with his bloody entrails oozing from his torn flank. He lifted his head with a feeble twisting motion.

'Marena,' he said with an effort, 'Marena. . . .' He did not recognize her. His voice failed.

There was a loud careless rustling in the bushes by the meadow. Marena bent her head towards Gobo. 'He's coming,' she whispered frantically. 'Gobo, He's coming. Can't you get up and come with me?'

Gobo lifted his head again feebly with a writhing motion, beat convulsively with his hoofs and then lay still.

With a crackling, snapping and rustling, He parted the bushes and stepped out.

Marena saw Him from quite near. She slunk slowly back, disappearing through the nearest bushes, and hastened to Bambi and Faline.

She looked back once again and saw how He was bending over and seizing the wounded deer.

Then they heard Gobo's wailing death shriek.

BAMBI was alone. He walked beside the water that ran swiftly among the reeds and swamp-willows.

He went there more and more often now that he was staying by himself. There were few trails there, and he hardly ever met any of his friends. That was just what he wanted. For his thoughts had grown serious and his heart heavy. He did not know what was happening within him. He did not even think about it. He merely recalled things aimlessly, and his whole life seemed to have become darker.

He used to stand for hours on the bank. The current, that flowed round a gentle bend there, occupied his entire thought. The cool air from the ripples brought him strange, refreshing, acrid smells that aroused forgetfulness and a sense of trust in him.

Bambi would stand and watch the ducks paddling companionably together. They talked

179

endlessly to one another in a friendly serious capable way.

There were a couple of mother ducks, each with a flock of young ones around her. They were constantly teaching their young ones things. And the little ones were always learning them. Sometimes one or the other of the mothers would give a warning. Then the young ducks would dash off in all directions. They would scatter and glide away perfectly noiselessly. Bambi saw how the smallest ones, who could not fly yet, would paddle among the thick rushes without moving a stem that might betray them by swaying. He would see the small dark bodies creep here and there among the reeds. Then he could see nothing more.

Later one of the mothers would give a short call and in a flash they would all flock around her again. In an instant they would reassemble their flotilla and go on cruising quietly about as before. Bambi marvelled anew at it each time. It was a constant source of wonder to him.

After one such alarm, Bambi asked one of the mothers, 'What was it? I was looking closely and I didn't see anything.'

'It was nothing at all,' answered the duck.

Another time one of the children gave the signal, turning like a flash and staring through the reeds. Presently he came out on the bank where Bambi was standing.

'What was it?' Bambi asked the little thing. 'I didn't see anything.'

'There wasn't anything,' the young one replied, shaking its tail feathers in a grown-up way and carefully putting the tips of its wings in place. Then it paddled through the water again.

Nevertheless Bambi had faith in the ducks. He came to the conclusion that they were more watchful than he, that they heard and saw things more quickly. When he stood watching them, that ceaseless tension that he felt within himself at other times relaxed a little.

He liked to talk with the ducks, too. They didn't talk the nonsense that he so often heard from the others. They talked about the broad skies and the wind and about distant fields where they feasted on choice tidbits.

From time to time Bambi saw something that looked like a fiery streak in the air beside the brook. 'Srrrri!' the humming-bird would cry softly, darting past like a tiny whirring speck. There was a gleam of green, a glow of red, as he flashed by and was gone. Bambi was thrilled and wanted to see the bright stranger near to. He called to him.

'Don't bother calling him,' the moorhen said to Bambi from among the reed clumps, 'don't bother calling. He'll never answer you.'

'Where are you?' asked Bambi, peering among the reeds.

But the moorhen only laughed loudly from an entirely different place, 'Here I am. That cranky creature you just called to won't talk to anyone. It's useless to call him.'

'He's so handsome,' said Bambi.

'But bad,' the moorhen retorted from still another place.

'What makes you think him bad?' Bambi inquired.

The moorhen answered from an altogether different place, 'He doesn't care for anything or anybody. Let anything happen that wants to, he won't speak to anybody and never thanked anybody for speaking to him. He never gives anybody warning when there's danger. He's never said a word to a living soul.'

'The poor . . .' said Bambi.

The moorhen went on talking, and her cheery, piping voice sounded from the far side again. 'He probably thinks that people are jealous of his silly markings and doesn't want them to get too good a look at him.'

'Certain other people don't let you get a good look at them either,' said Bambi.

In a twinkling the moorhen was standing in front of him. 'There's nothing to look at in my case,' she said simply. Small and gleaming with water, she stood there in her sleek feathers, her trim figure restless, animated and satisfied. In a flash she was gone again.

'I don't understand how people can stand so long in one spot,' she called from the water. And added from the far side, 'It's tiresome and dangerous to stay so long in one spot.' Then from the

other side she cried gaily once or twice. 'You have to keep moving,' she cried happily, 'you've got to keep moving if you want to keep whole and hearty.'

A soft rustling in the grass startled Bambi. He looked around. There was a reddish flash among the bushes. It disappeared in the reeds. At the same time a sharp warm smell reached his nostrils. The fox had slunk by.

Bambi wanted to cry out and stamp on the ground as a warning. But the sedges rustled as the fox parted them in quick leaps. The water splashed and a duck screamed desperately. Bambi heard her wings flapping and saw her white body flash through the leaves. He saw how her wings beat the fox's face with sharp blows. Then it grew still.

At the same moment the fox came out of the bushes holding the duck in his jaws. Her neck hung down limply, her wings were still moving, but the fox paid no attention to that. He looked sidewise at Bambi with sneering eyes and crept slowly into the thicket.

Bambi stood motionless.

A few of the old ducks had flown up with a rush of wings and were flying around in helpless fright. The moorhen was crying warnings from all directions. The field-mice chirped excitedly in the bushes. And the young orphaned ducks splashed about the sedge, crying with soft voices.

The humming-bird flew along the bank.

'Please tell us,' the young ducks cried, 'please, tell us, have you seen our mother?'

'Srrri,' cried the humming-bird shrilly, and flew past sparkling, 'what has she got to do with me?'

Bambi turned and went away. He wandered through a whole sea of golden-rod, passed through a grove of young beeches, crossed through old hazel thickets until he reached the edge of the deep ditch. He roamed around it, hoping to meet the old stag. He had not seen him for a long while, not since Gobo's death.

Then he caught a glimpse of him from afar and ran to meet him. For a while they walked together in silence, then the old stag asked, 'Well, do they still talk about him the way they used to?'

Bambi understood that he referred to Gobo, and replied, 'I don't know. I'm nearly alone now.' He hesitated, 'But I think of him very often.'

'Really,' said the old stag, 'are you alone now?'

'Yes,' said Bambi expectantly, but the old stag remained silent.

They went on. Suddenly the old stag stopped. 'Don't you hear anything?' he asked.

Bambi listened. He didn't hear anything.

'Come,' cried the old stag, and hurried forward. Bambi followed him. The stag stopped again. 'Don't you hear anything yet?' he asked.

Then Bambi heard a rustling that he did not understand. It sounded like branches being bent down and repeatedly springing up again. Something was beating the earth dully and irregularly.

Bambi wanted to flee, but the old stag cried, 'Come with me,' and ran in the direction of the noise. Bambi at his side ventured to ask, 'Isn't it dangerous?'

'It's terribly dangerous,' the old stag answered mysteriously.

Soon they saw branches being pulled and tugged at from below and shaken violently. They went nearer and saw that a little trail ran through the middle of the bushes.

Friend Hare was lying on the ground. He flung himself from side to side and writhed. Then he lay still and writhed again. Each of his motions pulled the branches over him.

Bambi noticed a dark thread-like leash. It ran right from the branch to Friend Hare and was twisted around his neck.

Friend Hare must have heard someone coming for he flung himself wildly into the air and fell to the ground. He tried to escape and rolled, jerking and writhing in the grass.

'Lie still,' the old stag commanded. Then sympathetically, with a gentle voice that went to Bambi's heart, he repeated in his ear, 'Be easy, Friend Hare, it's I. Don't move now. Lie perfectly still.'

The Hare lay motionless flat on the ground. His throttled breath rattled softly in his throat.

The old stag took the branch between his teeth, and twisted it. He bent it down. Then he walked around putting his weight cunningly against it. He held it to the earth with his hoof and snapped it with a single blow of his antlers.

Then he nodded encouragingly to the Hare. 'Lie still,' he said, 'even if I hurt you.'

Holding his head on one side, he laid one prong of his antlers close to the Hare's neck and pressed into the fur behind his ear. He made an effort and nodded. The Hare began to writhe.

The old stag immediately drew back. 'Lie still,' he commanded, 'it's a question of life and death for you.' He began over again. The Hare lay still gasping. Bambi stood close by, speechless with amazement.

One of the old stag's antlers, pressing against the Hare's fur, had slipped under the noose. The old stag was almost kneeling and twisted his head as though he were charging. He drove his antlers deeper and deeper under the noose, which gave at last and began to loosen.

The Hare could breathe again and his terror

and pain burst from him instantly. 'E-e-h!' he cried bitterly.

The old stag stopped. 'Keep quiet!' he cried, reproaching him gently, 'keep quiet.' His mouth was close to the Hare's shoulder, his antlers lay with a prong between the spoon-like ears. It looked as if he had spitted the Hare.

'How can you be so stupid as to cry at this time?' he grumbled gently, 'do you want the fox to come? Do you? I thought not. Keep quiet then.'

He continued to work away, slowly exerting all his strength. Suddenly the noose broke with a loud snap. The Hare slipped out and was free, without realizing it for a moment. He took a step and sat down again dazed. Then he hopped away, slowly and timidly at first, then faster and faster. Presently he was running with wild leaps.

Bambi looked after him. 'Without so much as a thank you,' he exclaimed in surprise.

'He's still terrified,' said the old stag.

The noose lay on the ground. Bambi touched it gently. It creaked, terrifying Bambi. That was a sound such as he had never heard in the woods.

'He?' asked Bambi softly.

The old stag nodded.

They walked on together in silence. 'Take care when you're going along a trail,' said the old stag, 'test all the branches. Prod them on all sides of you with your antlers. And turn back at once if you hear that creak. And when you've shed your antlers be doubly cautious. I never use trails any more.'

Bambi sank into troubled thought.

'He isn't here,' he whispered to himself in profound astonishment.

'No, He's not in the forest now,' the old stag answered.

'And yet He is here,' said Bambi, shaking his head.

The old stag went on and his voice was full of bitterness. 'How did your Gobo put it . . . ? Didn't Gobo tell you He is all-powerful and all-good.'

'He was good to Gobo,' Bambi whispered.

The old stag stopped. 'Do you believe that, Bambi?' he asked sadly. For the first time he had called Bambi by his name.

'I don't know,' cried Bambi, hurt. 'I don't understand it.'

The old stag said slowly, 'We must learn to live and be cautious.'

ONE morning Bambi came to grief.

The pale grey dawn was just creeping through the forest. A milky-white mist was rising from the meadow and the stillness that precedes the coming of light was everywhere. The crows were not awake yet, nor the magpies. The jays were asleep.

Bambi had met Faline the night before. She looked sadly at him and was very shy.

'I'm so much alone now,' she said gently.

'I'm alone, too,' Bambi answered with some hesitation.

'Why don't you stay with me any more?' Faline asked sorrowfully, and it hurt him to see the gay and lively Faline so serious and downcast.

'I want to be alone,' he replied. And gently as he tried to say it, it sounded hard. He felt it himself.

Faline looked at him and asked softly. 'Do you love me still?'

'I don't know,' Bambi answered in the same tone.

She walked silently away from him, leaving him alone.

He stood under the great oak at the meadow's edge and peered out cautiously, drinking in the pure and odourless morning air. It was moist and fresh from the earth, the dew, the grass and the wet woods. Bambi breathed in great gulps of it. All at once his spirit felt freer than for a long time. He walked happily on to the mist-covered meadow.

Then a sound like thunder crashed.

Bambi felt a fearful blow that made him stagger.

Mad with terror, he sprang back into the thicket and kept running. He did not understand what had happened. He could not grasp a single idea. He could only keep running on and on. Fear gripped his heart so that his breath failed as he rushed blindly on. Then a killing pain shot through him, so that he felt that he could not bear it. He felt something hot running over his left shoulder. It was like a thin burning thread coming from where the pain shot through him. Bambi had to stop running. He was forced to walk slower. Then he saw that he was limping. He sank down.

It was comfortable just to lie there and rest.

'Up, Bambi! Get up!' the old stag was standing beside him and nudging his shoulder gently.

Bambi wanted to answer, 'I can't,' but the old stag repeated, 'Up! Up!' And there was such compulsion in his voice and such tenderness that Bambi kept silent. Even the pain that shot through him stopped for a minute.

Then the old stag said hurriedly and anxiously, 'Get up! You must get away, my son.' My son! The words seemed to have escaped him. In a flash Bambi was on his feet.

'Good,' said the old stag, breathing deeply and speaking emphatically, 'Come with me now and keep close beside me.'

He walked swiftly ahead. Bambi followed him, but he felt a burning desire to let himself drop to the ground, to lie still and rest.

The old stag seemed to guess it and talked to him without stopping. 'Now you'll have to bear every pain. You can't think of lying down now. You mustn't think of it even for a moment. That's enough to tire you in itself. You must save yourself; do you understand me, Bambi? Save yourself; or else you are lost. Just remember that He is behind you; do you understand, Bambi? And He will kill you without mercy. Come on. Keep close to me. You'll soon be all right. You must be all right.'

Bambi had no strength left to think with. The

pain shot through him at every step he took. It took away his breath and his consciousness. The hot trickle, burning his shoulder, seared him like some deep heartfelt trouble.

The old stag made a wide circle. It took a long time. Through his veil of pain and weakness, Bambi was amazed to see that they were passing the great oak again.

The old stag stopped and snuffed the ground. 'He's still here,' he whispered. 'It's He. And that's His dog. Come along. Faster!' They ran.

Suddenly the old stag stopped again. 'Look,' he said, 'that's where you lay on the ground.'

Bambi saw the crushed grasses where a wide pool of his own blood was soaking into the earth.

The old stag snuffed warily around the spot. 'They were here, He and His dog,' he said. 'Come along!' He went ahead slowly, snuffing again and again.

Bambi saw the red drops gleaming on the leaves of the bushes and the grass stems. 'We passed here before,' he thought. But he couldn't speak.

'Aha!' said the old stag, and seemed almost joyful, 'we're behind them now.'

He continued for a while on the same path. Then he doubled unexpectedly and began a new circle. Bambi staggered after him. They came to the oak again but on the opposite side. For the second time they passed the place where Bambi had fallen down. Then the old stag went in still another direction.

'Eat that,' he commanded suddenly, stopping and pushing aside the grasses. He pointed to a pair of short dark-green leaves growing close together near the ground.

Bambi obeyed. They tasted terribly bitter and smelt sickeningly.

'How do you feel now?' the stag asked after a while.

'Better,' Bambi answered quickly. He was suddenly able to speak again. His senses had cleared and his fatigue grew less.

'Let's move on again,' the old stag commanded after another pause. After Bambi had been following him for a long time he said, 'At last!' They stopped.

'The bleeding has stopped,' said the old stag, 'the blood's stopped flowing from your wound. It isn't emptying your veins now. And it can't betray you any more either. It can't show Him and His dog where to find you and kill you.'

The old stag looked worried and tired but his voice sounded joyful. 'Come along,' he went on, 'now you can rest.'

They reached a wide ditch which Bambi had never crossed. The old stag climbed down and Bambi tried to follow him. But it cost him a great effort to climb the steep slope on the farther side. The pain began to shoot violently through him again. He stumbled, regained his feet, and stumbled again, breathing hard.

'I can't help you,' said the old stag, 'you'll have to get up yourself.' Bambi reached the top. He felt the hot trickle on his shoulder again. He felt his strength ebbing for the second time.

'You're bleeding again,' said the old stag. 'I thought you would, but it's only a little,' he added in a whisper, 'and it doesn't make any difference now.'

They walked very slowly through a grove of lofty beeches. The ground was soft and level. They walked easily on it. Bambi felt a longing to lie down there, to stretch out and never move his limbs again. He couldn't go any further. His head ached. There was a humming in his ears. His nerves were quivering, and fever began to rack him. There was a darkness before his eyes. He felt nothing but a desire for rest and a detached amazement at finding his life so changed and shattered. He remembered how he had walked whole and uninjured through the woods that morning. It was barely an hour ago, and it seemed to him like some memory out of a distant, long-vanished past.

They passed through a scrub-oak and dog-wood thicket. A huge, hollow beech-trunk, thickly entangled with the bushes, lay right in front of them, barring the way.

'Here we are,' Bambi heard the old stag saying. He walked along the beech-trunk and Bambi walked beside him. He nearly fell into a hollow that lay in front of him.

'Here it is,' said the old stag at the moment; 'you can lie down here.'

Bambi sank down and did not move again.

The hollow was still deeper under the beech-trunk and formed a little chamber. The bushes closed thickly across the top so that whoever was within lay hidden.

'You'll be safe here,' said the old stag.

Days passed.

Bambi lay on the warm earth with the mouldering bark of the fallen tree above him. He felt his pain intensify and then grow less and less until it died away more and more gently.

Sometimes he would creep out and stand swaying weakly on his unsteady legs. He would take a few stiff steps to look for food. He ate plants now that he had never noticed before. Now they appealed to his taste and attracted him by their strange enticing acrid smell. Everything that he had disdained before and would spit out if it got accidentally into his mouth, seemed appetizing to him. He still disliked many of the little leaves and short, coarse shoots; but he ate them anyway as though he were compelled to, and his wound healed faster. He felt his strength returning.

He was cured, but he didn't leave the hollow yet. He walked around a little at night, but lay quietly on his bed by day. Not until the fever had entirely left his body did Bambi begin to think over all that had happened to him. Then a great terror awoke in him, and a profound tremor passed through his heart. He could not shake himself free of it. He could not get up and run about as before. He lay still and troubled. He felt terrified, ashamed, amazed and troubled by turns. Sometimes he was full of despair, at others of joy.

The old stag was always with him. At first he stayed day and night at Bambi's side. Then he left him alone at times, especially when he saw Bambi deep in thought. But he always kept close at hand.

One night there was thunder and lightning and a downpour of rain, although the sky was clear and the setting sun was streaming down. The blackbirds sang loudly in all the neighbouring tree-tops, the finches warbled, the field-mice chirped in the bushes. Among the grasses or from under the bushes, the metallic, throaty cackling of the pheasants sounded at intervals. The woodpecker laughed exultantly and the doves cooed their fervid love.

Bambi crept out of the hollow. Life was beautiful. The old stag was standing there as though he expected Bambi. They sauntered on together.

ONE night when the air was whispering with the autumnal fall of leaves the screech-owl shrieked piercingly among the branches. Then he waited.

But Bambi had spied him already through the thinning leaves, and stopped.

The screech-owl flew nearer and shrieked louder. Then he waited again. But Bambi did not say anything.

Then the owl could restrain himself no longer. 'Aren't you frightened?' he asked, displeased.

'Well,' Bambi replied, 'a little.'

'Is that so?' the screech-owl cooed in an offended tone. 'Only a little. You used to get terribly frightened. It was really a pleasure to see how frightened you'd get. But for some reason or other you're only a little frightened now.' He grew angrier and repeated, 'Only a little!'

The screech-owl was getting old, and that was why he was so much vainer and so much more sensitive than before.

Bambi wanted to answer, 'I wasn't ever frightened before either,' but he decided to keep that to himself. He was sorry to see the good old screech-owl sitting there so angry. He tried to soothe him. 'Maybe it's because I thought of you right away,' he said.

'What?' said the screech-owl, becoming happy again, 'you really did think of me?'

'Yes,' Bambi answered with some hesitation, 'as soon as I heard you screech. Otherwise, of course, I'd have been as scared as ever.'

'Really?' cooed the owl.

Bambi hadn't the heart to deny it. What difference did it make anyhow? Let the little old child enjoy himself.

'I really did,' he assured him, and went on, 'I'm so happy, for a thrill goes through me when I hear you so suddenly.'

The screech-owl fluffed up his feathers into a soft, brownish-grey, downy ball. He was happy. 'It's nice of you to think of me,' he cooed tenderly, 'very nice. We haven't seen each other for a long time.'

'A very long time,' said Bambi.

'You don't use the old trails any more, do you?' the screech-owl inquired.

'No,' said Bambi slowly, 'I don't use the old trails any more.'

'I'm also seeing more of the world than I used to,' the screech-owl observed boastfully. He didn't mention that he had been driven from his hereditary haunts by a pitiless younger rival. 'You can't stay for ever in the same spot,' he added. Then he waited for an answer.

But Bambi had gone away. By now he understood almost as well as the old stag how to disappear suddenly and noiselessly.

The screech-owl was provoked. 'It's a shame ...' he cooed to himself. He shook his feathers, sank his bill deep into his breast and silently philosophized, 'You should never imagine you can be friends with great folks. They can be as nice as pie, but when the time comes they haven't a thought for you, and you're left sitting stupidly by yourself as I'm sitting here now....'

Suddenly he dropped to the earth like a stone. He had spied a mouse. It squeaked once in his talons. He tore it to pieces, for he was furious. He crammed the little morsel faster than usual. Then he flew off. 'What do all your great folks mean to me?' he asked. 'Not a thing.' He began to screech so piercingly and ceaselessly that a pair of wood-doves whom he passed awoke and fled from their roost with loud wing-beats.

The storm swept the woods for several days and tore the last leaves from the branches. Then the trees stood stripped.

Bambi was wandering homewards in the grey

dawn in order to sleep in the hollow with the old stag.

A shrill voice called him once or twice in quick succession. He stopped. Then the squirrel scampered down from the branches in a twinkling and sat on the ground in front of him.

'Is it really you?' he shrilled, surprised and delighted. 'I recognized you the minute you passed me, but I couldn't believe . . .'

'Where did you come from?' asked Bambi.

The merry little face in front of him grew quite troubled. 'The oak is gone,' he began plaintively, 'my beautiful old oak, do you remember it? It was awful. He chopped it down.'

Bambi hung his head sadly. His very soul felt sorry for the wonderful old tree.

'As soon as it happened,' the squirrel related, 'everybody who lived in the tree fled and watched how He bit through the trunk with a gigantic flashing tooth. The tree groaned aloud when it was wounded. It kept on groaning and the tooth kept gnawing, it was dreadful to hear it. Then the poor beautiful tree fell out on the meadow. Everybody cried.'

Bambi was silent.

'Yes,' sighed the squirrel, 'He can do anything. He's all-powerful.' He gazed at Bambi out of his big eyes, and pointed his ears. But Bambi kept silent.

'Then we were all homeless,' the squirrel went
on. 'I don't even know where the others scattered
to. I came here. But I won't find another tree like
that in a hurry.'

'The old oak,' said Bambi to himself, 'I knew it
from the time I was a child.'

'O well,' said the squirrel. 'But to think it's
really you,' he went on delightedly. 'Everybody
said you must be dead long ago. Of course there
were some people now and then who said you
were still alive. Once in a while someone said he

203

had seen you. But nobody could find out anything definite. And so I thought it was only gossip,' the squirrel gazed at him inquisitively, 'since you didn't come back any more.'

Bambi could see how curious he was and how he was fishing for an answer.

Bambi kept silent. But a gentle anxious curiosity was stirring in him, too. He wanted to ask about Faline, about Aunt Ena, and Ronno and Karus, about all his childhood companions. But he kept silent.

The squirrel still sat in front of him, studying him. 'What antlers!' he cried admiringly. 'What antlers! Nobody in the whole forest, except the old Prince, has antlers like that.'

Once Bambi would have felt elated and flattered by such praise. But he only said, 'Maybe.'

The squirrel nodded quickly with his head. 'Really,' he said, surprised, 'you're beginning to get grey.'

Bambi wandered on.

Squirrel perceived that the conversation was over and sprang through the bushes. 'Good day,' he shouted down. 'Good-bye. I'm very glad I met you. If I see any of your acquaintances I'll tell them you're still alive. They'll all be glad.'

Bambi heard him and again felt that gentle stirring in his heart. But he said nothing. When he was still a child the old stag had taught him that you must live alone. Then and afterwards the old stag had revealed much wisdom and many secrets to him. But of all his teachings this had been the most important; you must live alone, if you wanted to preserve yourself, if you understood existence, if you wanted to attain wisdom, you had to live alone.

'But,' Bambi had once objected, 'we two are always together now.'

'Not for very much longer,' the old stag had answered quickly. That was a few weeks ago. Now it occurred to Bambi again, and he suddenly remembered how even the old stag's very first words to him had been about singleness. That day when Bambi was still a child calling for his mother, the old stag had come to him and asked him, 'Can't you stay by yourself?'

Bambi wandered on.

THE forest was again under snow, lying silent beneath its deep white mantle. Only the crows' calls could be heard. Now and then came a magpie's noisy chattering. The soft twittering of the field-mice sounded timidly. Then the frost hardened and everything grew still. The air began to hum with the cold.

One morning a dog's baying broke the silence.

It was a continuous hurrying bay that pressed on quickly through the woods, eager and clear and harrying with loud yelps.

Bambi raised his head in the hollow under the fallen tree, and looked at the old stag who was lying beside him.

'That's nothing,' said the old stag in answer to Bambi's glance, 'nothing that need bother us.'

Still they both listened.

They lay in their hollow with the old beech-trunk like a sheltering roof above them. The deep snow kept the icy draught from them, and the tangled bushes hid them from curious eyes.

The baying grew nearer. It was angry and panting and relentless. It sounded like the bark of a small hound. It came constantly closer.

Then they heard panting of another kind. They heard a low laboured snarling under the angry barking. Bambi grew uneasy, but the old stag quieted him again. 'We don't need to worry about it,' he said. They lay silent in their warm hollow and peered out.

The footsteps drew nearer and nearer through the branches. The snow dropped from the shaken boughs and clouds of it rose from the earth.

Through the snow and over the roots and branches, the fox came springing, crouching and slinking. They were right; a little, short-legged hound was after him.

One of the fox's fore-legs was crushed and the fur torn around it. He held his shattered paw in front of him, and blood poured from his wound. He was gasping for breath. His eyes were staring with terror and exertion. He was beside himself with rage and fear. He was desperate and exhausted.

Once in a while he would face around and snarl so that the dog was startled and would fall back a few steps.

Presently the fox sat down on his haunches. He could go no farther. Raising his mangled forepaw pitifully, with his jaws open and his lips drawn back, he snarled at the dog.

But the dog was never silent for a minute. His high, rasping bark only grew fuller and deeper. 'Here,' he yapped, 'here he is! Here! Here! Here!' He was not abusing the fox. He was not even speaking to him, but was urging someone on who was still far behind.

Bambi knew as well as the old stag did that it was He the dog was calling.

The fox knew it too. The blood was streaming down from him and fell from his breast into the snow, making a fiery red spot on the icy white surface, and steaming slowly.

A weakness overcame the fox. His crushed foot sank down helpless, but a burning pain shot through it when it touched the cold snow. He lifted it again with an effort and held it quivering in front of him.

'Let me go,' said the fox, beginning to speak, 'let me go.' He spoke softly and beseechingly. He was quite weak and despondent.

'No! No! No!' the dog howled.

The fox pleaded still more insistently. 'We're relations,' he pleaded, 'we're brothers almost. Let me go home. Let me die with my family at least. We're brothers almost, you and I.'

'No! No! No!' the dog raged.

Then the fox rose so that he was sitting perfectly erect. He dropped his handsome pointed muzzle on his bleeding breast, raised his eyes and looked the dog straight in the face. In a completely altered voice, restrained and embittered, he growled, 'Aren't you ashamed, you traitor!'

'No! No! No!' yelped the dog.

But the fox went on, 'You turncoat, you renegade.' His maimed body was taut with contempt and hatred. 'You spy,' he hissed, 'you blackguard, you track us where He could never find us. You betray us, your own relations, me who am almost your brother. And you stand there and aren't ashamed!'

Instantly many other voices sounded loudly round about.

'Traitor!' cried the magpie from the tree.

'Spy!' shrieked the jay.

'Blackguard!' the weasel hissed.

'Renegade!' snarled the ferret.

From every tree and bush came chirpings, peepings, shrill cries, while overhead the crows cawed, 'Spy! Spy!' Everyone had rushed up, and from the trees or from safe hiding places on the ground, they watched the contest. The fury that had burst from the fox released an embittered anger in them all. And the blood spilt on the snow, that steamed before their eyes, maddened them and made them forget all caution.

The dog stared around him. 'Who are you?' he

yelped. 'What do you want? What do you know about it? What are you talking about? Everything belongs to Him, just as I do. But I, I love Him. I worship Him, I serve Him. Do you think you can oppose Him, poor creatures like you? He's all powerful. He's above all of you. Everything we have comes from Him. Everything that lives or grows comes from Him.' The dog was quivering with exaltation.

'Traitor!' cried the squirrel shrilly.

'Yes, traitor!' hissed the fox. 'Nobody is a traitor but you, only you.'

The dog was dancing about in a frenzy of devotion. 'Only me?' he cried, 'you lie. Aren't there many many others on His side? The horse, the cow, the sheep, the chickens, many, many of you and your kind are on His side and worship Him and serve Him.'

'They're rabble,' snarled the fox, full of a boundless contempt.

Then the dog could contain himself no longer and sprang at the fox's throat. Growling, spitting, and yelping, they rolled in the snow, a writhing, savagely snapping mass from which fur flew. The snow rose in clouds and was spattered with fine drops of blood. At last the fox could not fight any more. In a few seconds he was lying on his back, his white belly uppermost. He twitched and stiffened and died.

The dog shook him a few times, then let him fall on the trampled snow. He stood beside him, his legs planted, calling in a deep, loud voice, 'Here! Here! He's here!'

The others were horror-struck and fled in all directions.

'Dreadful,' said Bambi softly to the old stag in the hollow.

'The most dreadful part of all,' the old stag answered, 'is that the dogs believe what the hound just said. They believe it, they pass their lives in fear, they hate Him and themselves and yet they'd die for His sake.'

THE cold broke, and there was a warm spell in the middle of the winter. The earth drank great draughts of the melting snows, so that wide stretches of soil were everywhere visible. The blackbirds were not singing yet, but when they flew from the ground where they were hunting worms, or when they fluttered from tree to tree, they uttered a long-drawn joyous whistle that was almost a song. The woodpecker began to chatter now and then. Magpies and crows grew more talkative. The field-mice chirped more cheerily. And the pheasants, swooping down from their roosts, would stand in one spot preening their feathers and uttering their metallic throaty cacklings.

One such morning Bambi was roaming around as usual. In the grey dawn he came to the edge of the hollow. On the farther side where he had lived before something was stirring. Bambi stayed hidden in the thicket and peered across. A deer was wandering slowly to and fro, looking for places where the snow had melted, and cropping whatever grasses had sprung up so early.

Bambi wanted to turn at once and go away, for he recognized Faline. His first impulse was to spring forward and call her. But he stood as though rooted to the spot. He had not seen Faline for a long time. His heart began to beat faster. Faline moved slowly as though she were tired and sad. She resembled her mother now. She looked as old as Aunt Ena, as Bambi noticed with a strangely pained surprise.

Faline lifted her head and gazed across as though she sensed his presence. Again Bambi started forward, but he stopped again, hesitating and unable to stir.

He saw that Faline had grown old and grey.

'Gay, pert little Faline, how lovely she used to be,' he thought, 'and how lively!' His whole youth suddenly flashed before his eyes. The meadow, the trails where he walked with his mother, the happy games with Gobo and Faline, the nice grasshoppers and butterflies, the fight with Karus and Ronno when he had won Faline for his own. He felt happy again, and yet he trembled.

Faline wandered on, her head drooped to the ground, walking slowly, sadly and wearily away. At that moment Bambi loved her with an overpowering, tender melancholy. He wanted to rush through the hollow that separated him from the others. He wanted to overtake her, to talk with her, to talk to her about their youth and about everything that had happened.

He gazed after her as she went off, passing under the bare branches till finally she was lost to sight.

He stood there a long time staring after her.

Then there was a crash like thunder. Bambi shrank together. It came from where he was standing. Not even from a little way off but right beside him.

Then there was a second thunderclap, and right after that another.

Bambi leaped a little farther into the thicket, then stopped and listened. Everything was still. He glided stealthily homewards.

The old stag was there before him. He had not lain down yet, but was standing beside the fallen beech-trunk expectantly.

'Where have you been so long?' he asked, so seriously that Bambi grew silent.

'Did you hear it?' the old stag went on after a pause.

'Yes,' Bambi answered, 'three times. He must be in the woods.'

'Of course,' the old stag nodded, and repeated with a peculiar intonation, 'He is in the woods and we must go.'

'Where?' the word escaped Bambi.

'Where He is now,' said the old stag, and his voice was solemn.

Bambi was terrified.

'Don't be frightened,' the old stag went on, 'come with me and don't be frightened. I'm glad that I can take you and show you the way . . .' he hesitated and added softly, 'before I go.'

Bambi looked wonderingly at the old stag. And suddenly he noticed how aged he looked. His head was completely grey now. His face was perfectly gaunt. The deep light was extinguished in his eyes, and they had a feeble, greenish lustre and seemed to be blind.

Bambi and the old stag had not gone far before they caught the first whiff of that acrid smell that sent such dread and terror to their hearts.

Bambi stopped. But the old stag went on directly towards the scent. Bambi followed hesitantly.

The terrifying scent grew stronger and stronger. But the old stag kept on without stopping. The idea of flight sprang up in Bambi's mind and tugged at his heart. It seethed through his mind and body, and nearly swept him away. But he kept a firm grip on himself and stayed close behind the old stag.

Then the horrible scent grew so strong that it drowned out everything else, and it was hardly possible to breathe.

'Here He is,' said the old stag, moving to one side.

Through the bare branches, Bambi saw him lying on the trampled snow a few steps away.

An irresistible burst of terror swept over Bambi and with a sudden bound he started to give in to his impulse to flee.

'Halt!' he heard the old stag calling. Bambi looked around and saw the stag standing calmly where He was lying on the ground. Bambi was amazed and, moved by a sense of obedience, a boundless curiosity and quivering expectancy, he went closer.

'Come near,' said the old stag, 'don't be afraid.'

He was lying with his pale, naked face turned upwards, his hat a little to one side on the snow. Bambi, who did not know anything about hats, thought His horrible head was split in two. The poacher's shirt, open at the neck, was pierced where a wound gaped like a small red mouth. Blood was oozing out slowly. Blood was drying on his hair and around his nose. A big pool of it lay on the snow, which was melting from the warmth.

'We can stand right beside Him,' the old stag began softly, 'and it isn't dangerous.'

Bambi looked down at the prostrate form whose limbs and skin seemed so mysterious and terrible to him. He gazed at the dead eyes that stared up sightlessly at him. Bambi couldn't understand it all.

'Bambi,' the old stag went on, 'do you remember what Gobo said and what the dog said, what they all think, do you remember?'

Bambi could not answer.

'Do you see, Bambi,' the old stag went on, 'do you see how He's lying there dead, like one of us? Listen, Bambi. He isn't all-powerful as they say. Everything that lives and grows doesn't come from Him. He isn't above us. He's just the same as we are. He has the same fears, the same needs, and suffers in the same way. He can be killed like us, and then He lies helpless on the ground like all the rest of us, as you see Him now.'

There was a silence.

'Do you understand me, Bambi?' asked the old stag.

'I think so,' Bambi said in a whisper.

'Then speak,' the old stag commanded.

Bambi was inspired, and said, trembling, 'There is Another who is over us all, over us and over Him.'

'Now I can go,' said the old stag.

He turned away, and they wandered side by side for a stretch.

Presently the old stag stopped in front of a tall oak. 'Don't follow me any farther, Bambi,' he began with a calm voice, 'my time is up. Now I have to look for a resting-place.'

Bambi tried to speak.

'Don't,' said the old stag, cutting him short, 'don't. In the hour which I am approaching we are all alone. Good-bye, my son. I loved you dearly.'

Dawn of the summer's day came hot, without a breath of wind or the usual morning chill. The sun seemed to come up faster than usual. It rose swiftly and flashed like a torch with dazzling rays.

The dew on the meadows and bushes was drawn up in an instant. The earth was perfectly dry so that the clods crumbled. The forest had been still from an early hour. Only a woodpecker hammered now and then, or the doves cooed their tireless, fervid tenderness.

Bambi was standing in a little clearing, forming a narrow glade in the heart of the thicket.

A swarm of midges danced and hummed around his head in the warm sunshine.

There was a low buzzing among the leaves of the hazel bushes near Bambi, and a big may-beetle crawled out and flew slowly by. He flew among the midges, up and up, till he reached the tree-top where he intended to sleep till evening. His wing-covers folded down hard and neatly and his wings vibrated with strength.

The midges divided to let the may-beetle pass through, and closed behind him again. His dark brown body, over which shone the vibrant glassy shimmer of his whirring wings, flashed for a moment in the sunshine as he disappeared.

'Did you see him?' the midges asked each other.

'That's the old may-beetle,' some of them hummed.

Others said, 'All of his offspring are dead. Only one is still alive. Only one.'

'How long will he live?' a number of midges asked.

The others answered, 'We don't know. Some of his offspring live a long time. They live for ever almost. . . . They see the sun thirty or forty times; we don't know exactly how many. Our lives are long enough, but we see the daylight only once or twice.'

'How long has the old beetle been living?' some very small midges asked.

'He has outlived his whole family. He's as old as the hills, as old as the hills. He's seen more and been through more in this world than we can even imagine.'

Bambi walked on. 'Midge buzzings,' he thought, 'midge buzzings.'

A delicate frightened call came to his ears.

He listened and went closer, perfectly softly,

keeping among the thickest bushes, and moving noiselessly as he had long known how to do.

The call came again, more urgent, more plaintively. Fawns' voices were wailing, 'Mother! Mother!'

Bambi glided through the bushes and followed the calls.

Two fawns were standing side by side, in their little red coats, a brother and sister, forsaken and despondent.

'Mother! Mother!' they called.

Before they knew what had happened Bambi was standing in front of them. They stared at him speechlessly.

'Your mother has no time for you now,' said Bambi severely.

He looked into the little brother's eyes. 'Can't you stay by yourself?' he asked.

The little brother and sister were silent.

Bambi turned and, gliding into the bushes, disappeared before they had come to their senses. He walked along.

'The little fellow pleases me,' he thought, 'perhaps I'll meet him again when he's larger. . . .'

He walked along. 'The little girl is nice too,' he thought. 'Faline looked like that when she was a fawn.'

He went on, and vanished in the forest.

Rudyard Kipling
The Jungle Book £1.95

Full of unforgettable characters – Mowgli, the boy abandoned in the jungle and raised by the wolf pack; Kaa, the rock python whose dance mesmerized even Baloo and Bagheera; Rikki-Tikki-Tavi, the brave mongoose who fought and killed the big black cobra; and more . . .

The magical stories in *The Jungle Book* have enchanted generations since they were first published nearly 100 years ago. Wonderful fairy tales, they will be much appreciated when read aloud to younger children.

Just So Stories £1.95

How the Elephant's Child had his nose pulled by the Crocodile; how the Rhinoceros got his skin and a very bad temper; how the Leopard, in a spot, took the Wise Bavarian's advice and got spots . . .

The *Just So Stories*, originally told to his daughter, are among Kipling's finest. Witty and inventive, they include illustrations full of hidden jokes and puzzles by the author himself.

Colin Dann
The Animals of Farthing Wood £2.50

Farthing Wood is threatened . . . man is moving in with bulldozers. The animals are desperate, their homes are destroyed and their very survival is at stake. Can they escape? Will fox and badger lead them to the safety of a new home? The journey is difficult and dangerous . . . can fox and badger keep the animals together? Will they all survive to find peace and happiness?

All these books are available at your local bookshop or newsagent, or can be ordered direct from the publisher. Indicate the number of copies required and fill in the form below.

Send to: **CS Department, Pan Books Ltd., P.O. Box 40, Basingstoke, Hants. RG21 2YT.**

or phone: 0256 469551 (Ansaphone), quoting title, author and Credit Card number.

Please enclose a remittance* to the value of the cover price plus 60p for the first book plus 30p per copy for each additional book ordered to a maximum charge of £2.40 to cover postage and packing.

*Payment may be made in sterling by UK personal cheque, postal order, sterling draft or international money order, made payable to Pan Books Ltd.

Alternatively by Barclaycard/Access:

Card No.

Signature:

Applicable only in the UK and Republic of Ireland.

While every effort is made to keep prices low, it is sometimes necessary to increase prices at short notice. Pan Books reserve the right to show on covers and charge new retail prices which may differ from those advertised in the text or elsewhere.

NAME AND ADDRESS IN BLOCK LETTERS PLEASE:

....

Name —————————————————————————

Address —————————————————————————

—————————————————————————

—————————————————————————

—————————————————————————

3/87